Miracle on the 17th Green

Miracle on the 17th Green

a novel by

James Patterson and Peter de Jonge

LITTLE, BROWN AND COMPANY
New York   Boston

Back Bay Books / Little, Brown and Company
Time Warner Book Group
1271 Avenue of the Americas, New York, NY 10020
Visit our Web site at www.twbookmark.com

First Edition

The characters and events in this book are fictitious. Any similarity to real
persons, living or dead, is coincidental and not intended by the author.

Interior and cover art by Scott McKowen

ISBN 0-316-69331-6 (hc) / 0-316-69335-9 (pb)
Library of Congress Control Number 96-77743

10   9   8   7

Q-FF

Printed in the United States of America

For Matthew and Joseph.

For the good folks of Toms River

and Sleepy Hollow.

Part 1

A Little Noise
from Winnetka

Chapter 1

It was Christmas morning and a balmy 38 degrees. In other words, a perfect day for golf, and there I stood on the semifrozen mud of the 17th tee at the Creekview Country Club in Winnetka, Illinois.

My marriage was disintegrating. My three kids, whom I love more than life itself, didn't know what to make of me lately, and I had a terrible feeling that come January, I was going to be fired from my job at Leo Burnett. Who knows, if everything went as badly as it possibly could, there was a chance I might be one of the homeless after that.

Ho! Ho! Ho!

I bent down, teed up an old scuffed Titleist, and squinted through the wind at the long tight par 5, lined on both sides by towering black leafless elms.

Now what follows is one of those mystical, largely unexplainable, out-of-body experiences, so please bear with me. Or as Vin Scully used to say at the start of his golf telecasts, pull up a chair and make yourself comfortable. I admit that in sheer unlikelihood, this probably ranks right up there with Truman upsetting Dewey, *It's a Wonderful Life*, and John Daly winning the British Open.

What can I say? Stuff happens to people. Tragedies befall saints. Fortune smiles on cretins. Extraordinary things happen to ordinary people. And this happened to me.

Since it is such a crucial number in this story, I should point out that I was starting my round on 17. Despite the unseasonable thaw, it *was* Christmas, the course was empty, and 17 just happened to be the tee closest to where I parked. Anyway, I knocked the cover off my drive.

Nothing unusual about that. I hit the ball farther than the pro here at Creekview. I even hit the ball farther than the current champ, Mark Duffel, who's twenty.

I trudged down the fairway, nudged my ball away from a sprinkler head, and hit my second shot, a 185-yard, 5-iron, stiff. Suddenly, I was feeling better. To hell with my problems. Golf can have that effect.

Now, here comes the weird part. This is where everything gets a little spooky, and I took my first step on this road — either to salvation or damnation.

I stroked that putt so clean and solid.

Strange.

I put such a pure sweet roll on it, the ball traveled over the grass like a bead of mercury rolls across the floor after you break a thermometer.

The beginning of a miracle. A harbinger. A sign.

The little white ball dropped into the little white cup for eagle.

I was hooked.

I was elated.

I was doomed.

I must tell you right now however, that this isn't the so-called Miracle on 17. Not even close.

I hurried to the next tee.

Chapter 2

I know what you're thinking. What's the big deal about a nine-foot putt in a practice round on a deserted golf course in the dead of winter, with the only witness a skinny red squirrel who had hopped onto the green in search of an acorn or two?

Let me give you a little quick background.

Except for tap-ins and your basic no-account three- or four-footers, I don't make putts less than twelve feet. My nickname, borrowed in a most unflattering way from the former world welterweight champion Roberto Duran, is "Hands of Stone." In spite of that, I've been club champ here at the Creekview Country Club in Winnetka five out of the past twelve years.

But it wasn't just that the putt on 17 went in. Everybody gets lucky sometime.

It was *how* the putt went in.

It didn't creep in the side door, or dribble in the front, or start off-line and get corrected by a spike mark. It was dead center from the instant it touched off my blade until it rammed home with all the subtlety of a Shaquille O'Neal dunk.

But even more important was the *feeling* I had as I stood over the putt. *I knew it was going in.*

Knew it in my hands, shoulders, legs, and bones.

Knew it with a degree of certainty that was almost spooky.

It was like something that had already happened, and all I had to do was patiently wait for the present to catch up.

For the first time in forty years, I could actually *see the line*. My nickname notwithstanding, my putting problem was never really my touch. It was in my eyes, or somewhere behind them in the plumbing of my brain. Does it break three inches or two? Does it break at the beginning or the end? Your guess was as good as mine.

But that morning as I stood with my eyes directly over the Titleist logo, my putting dyslexia was cured. It was as if someone from the Winnetka Highway Department had painted a dotted white line between my ball and the hole. Or better yet, had laid a small stretch of track about the size of my younger son, Noah's, train set, and all I had to do was get the ball started right and then watch it roll as if it were on rails into the center of the cup.

But, as I said before, this isn't the miracle I'm trying to tell you about.

Chapter 3

Like a middle-aged man who suddenly discovers Santa Claus is real after all, I raced to the next hole. I thumbed a tee into the cold dirt and smacked another solid drive out over the deserted course.

For the next few hours, I raced around the blighted landscape in a birdie-feeding frenzy.

After rolling in a fifteen-footer on 18, I jogged back over to 1 and played a full eighteen, then another nine, then nine more. In thirty-eight holes, I one-putted twenty-nine greens, had twenty birdies, and in four nines didn't post a score above 33. Time seemed to stand still.

During one unconscious stretch, where I birdied four holes in a row, my heart started beating so fast I had to lean against a tree and make myself take a few slow breaths.

I was afraid I was going to keel over and buy the farm right then, cut down — as it were — in my prime. And I don't know what would have annoyed me more — dying, or dying before I had a chance to tell anybody about these scores.

But my reverie was suddenly broken.

Standing on the 16th green for the third time that day, I happened to look out over the evergreens beside the fairway. There, wafting above the treeline, tethered to a nearby house, was a helium-filled Santa balloon.

In a panic, I fished my watch out of my bag. It turns out time hadn't stood still at all. It had kept right on ticking.

As I stood marooned in the middle of the course, a brisk fifteen-minute walk from my Jeep, a reckless fifteen-minute ride from my home, I was already *two hours and twenty minutes late for my own Christmas dinner.* Throwing the bag over my shoulder, I took off across the empty course like a Yellowstone camper pursued by a nasty bear looking for *its* Christmas dinner.

Or a man who had just seen a ghost. The ghost of Christmas past.

Chapter 4

My family is not the kind that any man in his right mind stands up for Christmas dinner, or any other meal or occasion. But then whose is?

Sarah, my wife, is generous, funny, frighteningly accomplished, and stunning, and I have been hopelessly in love with her for thirty years. She is the leading obstetrician in Winnetka, and for the past eight years has been an adjunct professor at the University of Chicago Medical School. She has always earned more than I have as a sort of midlevel advertising copywriter for Leo Burnett, but, at least until recently, neither one of us seemed to mind.

Our kids, to use one of Noah's current favorite words are "the bomb." That's *good*, by the way. They are also sensitive, caring, beautiful, and brilliant. They take after Sarah.

Elizabeth, born the year after we got married, is really only a kid to me. That she is in fact twenty-seven now is something I always have a hard time believing. It doesn't fit with the indelible image of the first time I held her, seconds after her birth. Then again, neither did her first date, her second, her third, and her high school and college graduations. A doctor herself now, she is in her second year of a radiology internship at Yale.

Simon, a junior in high school, is probably my closest friend in the world — though we've been testing that relationship lately. The kid is just so alive and honest. He's a pure flame. Although he has never been interested in golf, he's also the family's only other jock. One of the top high school soccer players in the state, he has been invited to travel with the National Junior Team next fall.

Last, but definitely not least, is our great philosopher-king, Noah, who arrived unexpectedly four years ago, and whose absurd verbal precociousness has been causing jaws to drop practically ever since. Statistically, I guess he's a genius, but what really kills me about him is his ferocious loyalty to his older brother.

One day last fall, Simon surprised us at supper by arriving with three gold loops dangling from his right earlobe. His mother and I were not exactly congratulating him on his new look.

After about five minutes, Noah stood up and announced, "If you two don't stop it, I'm eating in my room." Then he looked at us, shrugged his shoulders, and said, "Besides, what's the big deal? He's a teenager." I'm not making this up. He's four years old.

Of course, Simon feels the same way about Noah. In fact, we're all pretty much crazy about one another, with the very possible exception lately of Sarah toward me. What's caused her to lose affection for me? I can't say for sure. She refuses to talk about it anymore.

If I don't get it by now I never will, she says.

What I do understand is that I've been in a rut, a rut that keeps getting deeper and deeper, and she's tired of what must seem like the Sisyphean task of pulling me out of it. As she put it once, "I already have three kids. I don't want to be married to one." The fact is she's doing great, and I'm not doing much of anything, I guess, except bringing her down. She also says I'm cynical about her friends, and she's probably right.

On the other hand, maybe I never deserved her in the first place, and it just took her twenty-eight years to figure that out.

At any rate, what I had just done on Christmas afternoon wasn't likely to heal and soothe.

Chapter 5

When I finally walked into the kitchen, I was actually met by *five* pairs of angry eyes. I don't believe I mentioned Boris, our black-and-brown Welsh terrier, who also joined the group scowl, and may even have growled. This wasn't the first time I had faced this particular mob. I had let them down before, so much so that Simon had dubbed me the "late" Travis McKinley.

"Merry Christmas," offered Sarah, with exactly as much warmth and genuine Yuletide spirit as I deserved.

"I know it's inexcusable," I blurted, "I'm sorry. When I looked at my watch, I swear I couldn't believe it."

"No big deal, Old Man," said Elizabeth, who had flown in from New Haven the night before. "All you did is miss Christmas dinner."

"You're being too hard on the guy, Liz," said Simon, bristling with the kind of wounded sarcasm only a seventeen-year-old can muster, "He's just in that mild funk again. You know, the one he's been in since Armstrong walked on the moon."

Because we identified with each other so closely, I realize now that my long slump had hurt Simon at least as much as me. If I'd got my act together a little sooner, maybe he wouldn't have three holes in his right ear. Maybe he wouldn't have been suspended two days this fall for getting in a fistfight in the hallway with some goon on the football team. But Simon's going to be all right, I swear it.

"Don't worry," said Noah, who hates to see anyone looking miserable, "there'll be another one in exactly three hundred sixty-five days."

"Oh, I wouldn't be so sure of that," said Sarah. "At least not one that you're invited to."

I stood there with my face covered with mud and sweat, and dried blood where a branch had scraped my chin as I sprinted back through the woods. I stared hopelessly at Sarah, who was wearing a simple black dress and had her hair pulled back. She kept shaking her head, and the look on her face was about as pure as disgust can get.

"I know no one is going to believe this or be interested," I said, "but I was having a semireligious experience out there."

"What? You finally sunk a few putts?" snorted Elizabeth, provoking laughter all around and a particularly merry approving glance from her mom.

When am I going to learn to keep my moronic mouth shut? I asked myself in despair. The only good news was that my mad sprint through the woods had got me home in time to do the dishes and clean up. Noah, good soul that he is, stayed in the kitchen to help me dry. The work, and his company, temporarily took my mind off the paralyzing fear that I might eventually screw up one time too many and lose my place in this family.

Or maybe I already had.

Chapter 6

That night, the Midwest got blitzed by the first real snowstorm of the winter. The town Billy Sunday couldn't shut down, was.

Although I welcomed the closed offices and the temporary interruption in the flow of junk mail and bills, I was dying to get back on the course and find out if I could still see the line on my putts. Was my improvement permanent, or just a blip in the cosmos, a one-day Christmas gift from God?

It was five days before the snow had melted enough for me and my regular golfing buddies, Ron Claiborne, Joe Barreiro, and Charles Hall, to drive out to Medinah, one of the best courses in the country, where Ron's father-in-law was a member.

Medinah is a long, narrow, nasty test of golf. When it hosted the U.S. Open in 1990, the best score all week was a 67 by Hale Irwin.

That's exactly what I shot. With all the bonus payouts for greenies, birdies, sandies, presses, and double presses, my winnings were more than enough to buy lunch and drinks in the Men's Grill.

That afternoon, we had the place to ourselves. As we sat in one corner of the huge wood-paneled room, shooting the breeze and stewing in our ripe middle age, I picked up a spoon and banged it on Ron's half-empty Amstel Light.

"Gentlemen, I'm glad all of you are sitting down, because I have a rather shocking announcement," I said.

"You're getting a vasectomy," said Ron. "Congratulations."

"Talk about flogging a dead horse," said Joe.

"I'm going to the Senior Tour Qualifying School." I said, interrupting the high hilarity. "Starts two weeks from today in Tallahassee."

The silence was deafening. I'd been playing with these guys for twenty-five years. They were all top local amateurs and former college players, and until the sudden improvement in my putting, I don't even know if I was the best player at the table.

"It takes more than one sixty-seven to go up against Lee Trevino and Jimmy Colbert every week," said Ron finally. "You're completely out of your fucking mind, and that's putting it politely." It was almost as if he was angry.

"I appreciate your confidence," I said. "Really, I'm touched. I've broken par six nines in a row, and something wild has happened with my putting."

"No shit," said Joe.

"But that's not the point," I said. "The point is it's what I want to do, and for once before it's too late I'd like to know what it feels like to at least try to do what I want."

"You've already got the cushiest job in the Western World," said Joe. "You rotate the superlatives in McDonald's jingles. I mean, how many things can you come up with that rhyme with 'sesame seed bun'?"

"I hate it," I said with a vehemence that surprised even me. "And I've hated it every day for twenty-three years."

"Time sure does fly when you're having fun," said Charles.

"Listen," Joe said as he put a hand on my shoulder, "if you're really in trouble at the agency, call Stan Isaacs at the *Tribune*. He'd hire you in a second."

I groaned out loud. "I am in trouble at the agency. The word is they're canning twenty percent of the department. They're just waiting till after Christmas. But that still isn't the goddamn point."

"We can't seem to get the point, fellas," said Charles.

"I'm tired of groveling for the right to go on doing something I don't want to do in the first place. The other day I walked by Simon's room, where he was listening to some CD, and this angry grunge chant was coming through the door. Maybe I'm destined to be stuck in adolescence forever, but I knew *exactly* what those teenage mutant slackers meant. I know the life they're all afraid of — I'm living it."

"It's turtles," said Joe, "and by the way, Travis, what does the lovely and talented Sarah have to say about your sudden athletic ambitions?"

"Actually, I haven't told her," I said. *Confided* is probably the word I should have used.

Suddenly, three middle-aged men started laughing so hard that tears were soon streaming down their grizzled cheeks.

Not a word from any of them — just laughter. Not a believer in the bunch.

Chapter 7

The one and only reason Sarah and I went out for New Year's was that it would have taken too much devious and painful explaining to the kids not to. Particularly to Elizabeth, who, sensing something was wrong, had insisted on baby-sitting Noah, and practically shooed us out the front door.

"I feel like we just got fixed up," I said as we were backing out of the driveway. I was trying to keep things light.

"By our children instead of our parents," said Sarah. She was trying to keep things light, too.

Winnetka has a surprisingly good French restaurant, La Provence, in an elegant room at the top of the town's tallest office building, and that's where Sarah and I, teetering into our fourth decade together, went to ring in the New Year. That evening they were featuring a young retro singer from New Orleans, backed by a sextet, and dancing. The night was so cold and clear that from our corner table you could see the lights on the Canadian side of Lake Michigan.

I had planned to use our time together to tell Sarah about Q-School and my hopes of playing the Senior Tour. Instead, I found myself struggling to fill the awkward silences. And although I certainly had terribly important things to tell her, seeing her across from me so lovely and yet so distant made the other discussion seem almost irrelevant.

As I describe my problems with Sarah, I'm afraid you might get the impression that it was something I was able to harden myself against, or get used to, but that's not the way it felt. It was more like getting my heart broken, in a slightly different way, every day for two years. Maybe even longer than that.

Part of the problem, though I hate to admit it, is that I've come to feel like "Dr. McKinley's husband." I have been proud of Sarah and her ferocious competence since the day I met her. I really have. And it's not as if she thought she was marrying a future captain of industry. But the fact is, our careers have been going in opposite directions for quite a while now, and although I tell her it doesn't bother me, it does. The feeling of inequality has even found its way into our bedroom, if you know what I mean, where it hangs over our bed like one of those distorting funhouse mirrors.

Anyway, I want to fix it, not moan and groan about it. I just don't know how. Once one person starts feeling a little sorry for themselves in relationship to the other, it's tough. Because how can you talk about it with that person without feeling even more pathetic and insecure? This is excruciating. Can I stop now?

"Why are you staring at me?" Sarah eventually asked.

"Because you're beautiful," I said. Sarah, who wore a dark green velvet dress and gold earrings, did in fact look exquisite — but what I had really been doing was searching for some inkling of affection in her eyes. I needed to talk to her. I had some important things to say — to Sarah, and nobody else. But I didn't want to tell them to someone who would gaze at me like a stranger.

For so many years, I had been sure of her love. Sometimes it had been about the only thing I was certain of. *Well, if all else fails, Sarah will still love me.* Now that was as uncertain as everything else.

Nevertheless, as we ate and drank, we both relaxed. And almost in spite of ourselves, we began to enjoy each other's company

It reminded me how much I missed just talking to Sarah, how much I used to enjoy getting her phone calls during the day. Since men never grow up, at least with each other, Sarah was in many ways my only adult relationship, and I missed it badly.

After dinner the band started cranking out some of the great Cole Porter tunes, and as hard as the young would-be Sinatra tried to massacre them, the songs were just too good.

"We might as well dance," Sarah said. Maybe she didn't mean it to be cutting, but it was.

"And it's a slow dance," I said with a mock salaciousness that wasn't nearly as sarcastic as it pretended to be.

The band played "I Love Paris" and I held Sarah close for what seemed like the first time in months — because it was — and although she didn't exactly feel like she was mine, she felt really good.

I looked down at her hand, and I thought of the very first day of our honeymoon in California — when the surf had twisted her engagement ring off her finger. The ring had been lost, but Sarah had insisted that she didn't want to replace it. "Any other ring would make me feel like we're starting over," she said, "and we're not." It was exactly the kind of eccentric willfulness that I loved and admired Sarah for, but maybe it was also an omen.

And so perhaps was the fact that in the middle of our second dance Sarah's beeper went off. One of her patients had just gone into labor. She had to meet the young couple at the hospital in twenty-five minutes.

"Isn't someone covering for you tonight?" I asked, hoping I didn't sound too desperate. I hadn't told her about Q-School yet. I had to tell her. If anybody could understand, it would be Sarah. I mean, didn't we get together in the first place because we felt we could share our dreams?

"No, it's my turn," said Sarah, who had obviously volunteered for holiday duty. That was it. The party was over.

"Well, you've never looked prettier," I said with my bravest, dumbest half-smile. "Some little ginker is going to have a charmed life."

Sarah dropped me off at home on the way to the hospital.

"Happy New Year, Travis. Sorry," she managed.

"Yeah, me too," I said. "Happy New Year. Give my best to the new kid on the block."

I got out a bottle of Wild Turkey, and listened to Sinatra sing the damn songs right.

Then, I fell asleep on the couch, dreaming of a woman in a dark green dress with gold earrings, whom I missed talking to more than words can say.

Chapter 8

As the gleaming, chrome-plated elevator surged upward toward the twenty-eighth floor of the Chicago advertising monolith Leo Burnett and Company, I can't deny that I had a pleasant first-day-of-school feeling about being back.

There were no miracles to be had on the twenty-eighth floor, but who was I kidding anyway. I was way past the miracle stage in my career.

I suppose Burnett deserves some credit for trying so hard to seem like a friendly, homey place. There's the basket of shiny red apples in all the reception areas. The gift book at Christmas on a subject you might even be vaguely interested in. The signed card from the chairman on your birthday. But to be honest, the whole "just think of us as family" culture has always given me the willies, in the same way that a good hair weave is somehow even creepier than a bad rug.

For all the amenities, advertising for me has never been more than a job. Or a terrible mistake. A mistake I had never found a way to undo.

The insidious thing about advertising is that it requires so little productivity it can ruin you for any other kind of work. Have one pretty good idea a year, and you're a valuable cog in the wheel. Have one a month, and you walk on water. Except for politics, and maybe writing screenplays, in what other job can you go to work every day for five years, have literally nothing to show for it, and still get paid? Of course that's the trap. Because when your time is up, even the superstars of advertising have about four minutes to hold up in their defense. It's called a "reel," and mine is dated, dusty, maybe even moldy.

Still, I can't deny I've made a few good friends, and my best is the first guy I greet upon my return, Richard Bellistrano, who for the past ten years has been rattling the bars in the cage next to mine.

In addition to being the funniest person I've ever met, Richard has always extended like a generous Welcome mat the hospitable guarantee that no matter how bad I felt, he felt exponentially worse. Then again, misery and self-conscious torment are Richard's oxygen, his best and longest-running gag. Imagining Richard happy is like imagining a world where justice and merit prevailed. It's unthinkable. And although he has talked fervently about quitting every day since I've met him, I don't think he has seriously considered it for a nanosecond. Where else but in these unsacred halls could he be guaranteed to feel this stymied and fucked over?

"Good morning, Richard."

"Don't start with me," replied Richard, "I'm in a fetid humor."

"How were your holidays?" I ask.

"Have you seen *Nightmare on Elm Street Part Four*?"

I spent the morning working on a print ad for yet another new, tasty but healthy Kellogg's cereal — "Milk it for all it's worth" was probably my best effort — then I stepped out for lunch.

When I returned, Mike Kidd, the company's ponytailed wonderboy creative director, was sitting on my couch. This was not good. Had my visitor been the Grim Reaper himself it would have hardly been any worse. The chicken pot pie from lunch rose a few inches in my stomach.

Kidd's tiny Gucci-shod feet tapped involuntarily on my rug, although it was hard to tell if he was nervous or just excited. In any case, he got right to the point. That's Kidd's style, his strength, as it were.

"Travis, we're going to let you go," he said.

Like any other catastrophe, natural or otherwise, getting fired has a weird dreamlike quality to it. The suddenness. The devastating consequences. The finality.

Even though it was happening to me — To Me! — I was no more than a startled spectator, since all I could do was watch and listen, and wait for it to end.

I wish I could tell you that I was happy about it. After all, hating my job was one of the true passions of my life. I wish I was even a little grateful to have been given a much-needed push. But in fact I was scared shitless.

Suddenly all the fears that had kept me there so long were let loose inside my brain. Even with two incomes, we weren't saving enough.

What would we do now? By the time Noah was ready for college, tuition would probably be $100,000 a year. I barely took in a word as Kidd mumbled about my generous severance package, and the lovely service now available to me called "outplacement."

What made me bristle was that this sawed-off little bastard so clearly enjoyed what he was doing. Kidd obviously relished his exercise of power. Maybe it made him feel a little smarter. More attractive. A couple of inches taller.

I hadn't said a word for so long, even Kidd was starting to look uncomfortable on my couch. Maybe he'd noticed something in my expression. Not that I was going to pop him or anything. Even I had to admit this was not Mike Kidd's doing.

"So how long have you worked here?" he finally asked.

"Twenty-three years," I said. *Unbelievable to hear those words come out of my mouth.*

"Wow. I would have thought you'd be chairman by now. I just meant . . ."

"It's okay. It's fine, Mike."

"You must have started young. You can't be more than forty-two, forty-three."

"Actually, I'm fifty."

He got up from my couch. "Human Resources will have all the information you need, Travis." He shook my hand and left.

I was out of advertising.

I was free. I could do anything I wanted to.

Without saying a word to anyone or stopping at Personnel, I

grabbed my coat and headed outside. I barely had time to turn the corner before I doubled over and hurled my chicken pot pie against one of the shiny black stones at the base of the Leo Burnett and Company sign.

Ah, the sweet taste of freedom.

Chapter 9

What's that saying — be careful what you want, you just might get it?

Without thinking where I was going, I headed north on Clark, and without knowing why, except that throwing up almost always makes you feel better, my sense of doom started to lift.

I had a plan. Didn't I have a plan? I certainly needed a plan.

I was reminded how much I like this big wide-open city in the middle of America. There's nothing hip about it, nothing pretentious. It's a place with long hard winters and big beautiful summers, where people try their ass off, and as I humped past no-nonsense taverns, pizza parlors, coffee shops, and bookstores, a couple of weeks past fifty, somewhere in the middle of my life, I knew I still had a lot of try left in me.

Mike Kidd thought I looked forty-two. Hell, I could barely believe

I was fifty myself. I felt more like thirty-seven, or twenty-eight, or fourteen.

But no matter how I looked or felt, there was no denying that time was getting precious. The meter was running. And if I was going to do anything of consequence in this final third or whatever of my life, I had to get on with it.

As in now.

Without further deliberation, I went to an ATM. I transferred three thousand dollars from my savings account to my checking account.

I bought some envelopes, stamps, and sent my three-thousand-dollar Senior Q-School entry fee to the PGA office in Ponte Vedra Beach, Florida. That's what you're supposed to do when you get fired, isn't it? Spend three thousand dollars in the first hour just to get the blood flowing.

Then I went to a Greek coffee shop, where I wrote a long, emotional letter to Elizabeth. She had already headed back to New Haven. In the letter, I described the day I was having so far, my plans for the future, but mostly I told Elizabeth how much I loved her. I must have got choked up, because when I finally stood to pay, the waitresses were all looking at me funny.

Even after taking care of all this business, it was still only midafternoon. I caught an early train back to Winnetka. I picked up Noah at nursery school and the two of us went grocery shopping.

By the time Simon and Sarah got home I was ready for them with linguini and clam sauce, garlic bread, and a huge salad with three different kinds of lettuce, which happens to be one of Sarah's favorites.

I kept thinking: *I have to talk to Sarah. I need to talk to her.* And the fact that I still hadn't gave the meal a surreal, Last Supper quality.

"Isn't anyone wondering," I asked, as soon as they had a chance to take a couple of bites, "how on the first workday of the new year, I was able to get home so early that Noah and I had time to prepare this incredibly garlicky and delectable repast?"

"Dad did most of it," Noah piped in, "but I gave him something he called 'moral support.'"

"Okay, Travis," Sarah bit, "how is it that you got home so early?"

"Because I got fired, dear," I said, my voice cracking a little bit. "Would you like some more wine?"

"That would be lovely, Travis, but I didn't realize getting fired was a cause for celebration."

I took a deep breath. "You're right. Getting fired was just a prelude. This modest celebration is for what I have decided to do next."

"Which is what?" asked Simon.

I let out the breath I'd sucked in. "I'm going to Qualifying School. I'm going to try to make the Senior Tour. I think I have a real good shot."

"I thought you were done with school," said Noah.

"It's a school for grown-ups," I patiently explained.

"I wouldn't go that far," said Sarah.

I glanced at Sarah, and she gave me a look so piercing it might have been fatal if it weren't for the slightest hint of a smile.

I had wanted to tell her about Q-School on New Year's, but the fact that I hadn't called her this afternoon was undeniable evidence of how bad things had got between us.

"Travis, I have just one question," she said. "When, as you say, you get through this so-called Qualifying School, where do you want your mail forwarded to?"

Noah spoke up again. "Is that what they said at work, Dad, 'You're fired!' like in the cartoons?"

"Actually, the exact words were 'Travis, we're going to let you go.' . . . *Sarah, I tried to tell you*," I said to her.

"Were you asking them if you could go somewhere?" asked Noah.

"No, that's just the way they put it. It's called a euphemism."

"A upamism," tried Noah.

Sarah got up from the dinner table and left the room, while I continued to talk things over with the boys, answering their questions as best I could.

I explained, mainly to Noah since Simon was already pretty familiar with the concept, that Q-School was the name of this huge annual tournament in which the top eight finishers get to play for one year on the Senior Tour, a series of pro tournaments held all over the country almost every week for players fifty years and older. Most of the spots in this tour, I said, automatically go to players like Jack Nicklaus and Arnold Palmer and Lee Trevino, guys who were stars on the regular tour, but that every year there are these eight spots up for grabs — that theoretically, at least — anyone can win. Both of them lit up at the thought of their dad playing with the pros, particularly

Simon. It was as if the two of us were crawling out of our malaise together.

But Sarah and I apparently had nothing more to discuss, and that seemed to say it all.

Sad. It's going around these days, isn't it?

Chapter 10

The next afternoon, my ninety-two-year-old grandfather, Edwin Joseph McKinley, stood in the middle of the 12th fairway of the Creekview Country Club.

He dropped three Titleists onto the cold sod.

In deference to the 35-degree chill, he wore a red flannel shirt buttoned all the way up against the loose folds of his neck, a heavy cardigan and corduroys, a wool cap, boots, and a tan workcoat, like the kind he wore when he and a friend built my parents' house, the house I was born in, fifty-one years before.

About forty yards away, directly between us and the small green, was a large leafless oak.

"All right," said Pop with a gravelly voice worn thin but still full of purpose, "you got two eighteen to the front edge. On the first one, I want you to slice the ball around the tree."

I pulled out a 2-iron, took a deep breath and a brisk waggle, and hit a hard low cut that caught the right edge of the green.

"That'll play," said Pop. "Now, a hook."

With the same club and same basic swing, I drew the ball around the tree. Since my grandfather first introduced me to the game forty-two years ago, he has been my only teacher. He gave me my swing and my game and a great many other things at least as valuable. "There's no such thing as a straight ball" was one of his basic tenets. "If you're not shaping the shot, you're not playing golf."

If my relationship with my father, who died three years ago of a heart attack, was always complex and unsatisfying, my relationship with my grandfather has always been blood simple. I adored him, and he got a kick out of being adored. I loved everything about him and still do. His laugh, his scent, the touch of his skin, that he was a carpenter and a mechanic and never graduated from high school, and that he loved to fight.

The oldest brother and de facto bodyguard for an enormous farm family of eleven kids, my grandfather is both the toughest and the gentlest of men. Although in his later years he began shrinking and shedding pounds in bunches, as if his body, guided by an intelligence of its own, were streamlining itself for old age, in his prime he was about five feet nine and weighed 235 pounds and was the strongest man in Winnetka.

My younger son, Noah, has a fixation with action figures, particularly X-Men like Cyclops and Wolverine and Metalhead, and as a young boy my grandfather filled a similar need for me. I can describe in great detail each of his unscheduled bouts in a pugilistic career that started when he was eleven and ended in his late forties, but a characteristic tale was when as a twenty-year-old on his first foray into Chicago, in his brand-new Model A Ford, a cabbie, irked by his hesitant driving, yelled at him, "Go back to the farm!"

Since that was exactly where he'd come from, and where he would soon return, the suggestion was particularly nettlesome, although the driver would probably have met the same fate had he shouted something as generic as "I haven't got all day, pal!"

You see, not only is my grandfather a terrible driver, he brooks no criticism of it, from anyone but a blood relative.

So Pop put his car in park, walked back to the cabbie, and knocked him out through the window.

As a rail-thin, bespectacled, almost emaciated little kid, whose distant father seemed to have no discernible connection to the physical world, I latched on to these stories like a precious inheritance, often prompting him to retell this one or that one, and after every retelling my grandfather would tilt his head back and laugh, with a delight that was as pure and righteous and essentially modest as the snow that still covered this course in patches.

As a golf teacher, Pop was demanding. He introduced me to the game at eight, but wouldn't let me play my first round until I'd spent three years hitting balls on the driving range, and practicing on and around the putting green. And he always began our literally thousands of rounds together with the same terse but merry challenge — "No gimmes. No mulligans. No bullshit. Let's play golf."

But he always made it clear that his stringency was based on respect for both the game and me, and that if we went about it in the right and thorough manner, there was no limit to what I might be able to accomplish.

I suspect that whatever confidence I have as a person in this world is based directly on what, as a very young man on this very course, he gave me the opportunity to earn.

"The third shot is easy," he said. "Just hit the ball over the god-damned tree."

For a second, I was so overcome with affection for this nerveless old coot, I couldn't see the ball. How many more of these playing lessons would I have? Would this be the last? Time, as I said, was getting more and more precious. Although I can't say that's why my 2-iron crashed into the upper branches.

"Pop," I said, "I got fired yesterday."

"Well, you better learn how to hit the ball a little higher then."

"You're right about that," I said, "because I'm going to try to play the Senior Tour. You don't think I'm fooling myself, do you?"

"I think you've been fooling yourself for thirty years," he said. "I always thought you should try to play the tour, but your parents thought I was crazy. Too risky, they thought, so I stayed out of it."

"You don't think it's too late?"

"Christ, no. It's about time you try to make an honest living."

"Things haven't been too good with Sarah either," I said, figuring I might as well get it all out on the table.

"Could be related," Pop said. "A guy who hates his job isn't going to be too charming at home."

Part 2

The Miracle Tour

Chapter 11

If this were a movie, and hopefully it will be soon, the producers would buy an uptempo song like "Taking Care of Business, Working Overtime" and show a two-minute montage of me practicing furiously, progressing from utter ineptitude to a very tentative competence, as I prepared myself and my game for the Senior Tour Q-School. Sort of a charmingly geriatric version of Rocky sucking eggs and running the steps of the Philadelphia City Hall.

I didn't have time for that.

Two days later, I threw some clothes into an old suitcase, along with my birth certificate and a thousand dollars in traveler's checks. I grabbed my sticks and golf shoes and a handful of Sinatra and Tom Petty tapes.

Sarah drove me to O'Hare, and even gave me a kiss (on the cheek) before I passed through the metal detector. The night before we finally had an actual conversation, and I tried to explain how important it was for me to try this. I can't say she was happy about it, and she clearly wasn't enthused about the prospect of supporting our family if it didn't pan out, something she essentially felt she was doing already.

"Why couldn't you have tried this twenty-five years ago?" she asked at one point, and I didn't know quite how to tell her. Twenty-five years ago, even if I could putt, there was no way on earth I would have left Sarah and Elizabeth for a life in hotel rooms, but now, in a strange way, I almost had no choice.

"Good luck," she said. "You're going to make it, Travis." That was all. It wasn't exactly *Casablanca*, but it was more than I expected.

A few minutes later, I folded myself into a cheap seat for a night flight to Tampa. As I sat with my feet up against the droning bulwark and peered out the window at the lights of Chicago passing below, I thought of something my most precocious friend in high school liked to say: "When the going gets weird, the weird turn pro."

Maybe I was a self-deluded fool, who would soon be looking back on his three decades in the velvet yoke of advertising with nostalgic longing, but in the last couple of weeks things had certainly gotten a lot more interesting, and stranger, and I was about to turn pro.

In Tampa, I rented another cramped seat, this time in a very compact Chevy, and with Sinatra's "Come Fly with Me" and "Imagination" serving as twin anthems, I made the three-hour drive to Tallahassee, arriving just after midnight.

Q-School and the final round of the Eastern regional, which had also been wiped out by Hurricane Eunice, were being held at a large resort complex called the Tallahassee Dunes, and since I was still too worked up to sleep, I headed over to take a look.

The parking lot was enormous, and except for a row of tarp-covered golfing carts, completely empty. The lot's vast black landscape, cracked and potholed and greasy, seemed as lunar as the three-quarter moon.

I parked the car by the clubhouse, and walked over toward what I assumed was the 18th green.

I took in its tranquil amoeba shape. In the moonlight, the undulating short-cropped surface looked like a pond, and behind it the rest of the course receded beckoningly into semidarkness like a dream.

Without consciously deciding to do so, I wandered out into the dream.

Maybe it's because my grandfather wouldn't let me play my first round for three years, but for me a golf course has always been a kind of sacred roped-off place, where outside concerns are permitted to intrude only on my own terms. Ever since I was a kid, I have always felt like something of an outsider, but on a golf course I feel the opposite, the energy of the land itself coming up through my feet.

For the next hour and a half, I walked the entire course. There was just enough light for me to see that there was nothing plush or country-clubbish about this layout, just a threadbare tract of overplayed and underirrigated Florida scrub pine, but it had good bones, and I took an instant liking to it.

I liked the way it felt underfoot. This is where I make my stand, I thought to myself.

When I reached a wide-open stretch in the center of what I later learned was the 16th fairway, which like all the parts of all the other holes at the Dunes would become as intimate and crucial a part of my personal history as the street I grew up on, and the Chicago motel room in which I lost my virginity, I lay down on my back and stared up at the star-filled sky. I was searching the constellations for some portent of what was to come.

Would I be forgiven my still-unspecified sins, or was my marriage busted beyond any hope of repair? Was I about to lose the luxury of my delusions and come up hard against the limits of my talent and guts, or was a new and entirely better stage of my life about to begin?

As usual, the stars weren't giving away any plotlines.

When I started getting drowsy, I dusted myself off and headed back to the car to find a cheap place to stay. The first one I came to was a Motel 6, but that sounded way too much like a double bogey, so I registered instead at the Ben Franklin Motor Court, where I got a bed, a towel, and a bar of soap for twenty-one dollars a night.

Suddenly, my life seemed very simple. I was doing what my heart told me to do, and that couldn't be all wrong.

Chapter 12

Six hours later I was back at the course.

I wanted to have plenty of time to register and check in, scope out the practice range and the putting green, and then play a calm, relaxed practice round.

But at 7:45 A.M. the huge parking lot was already packed and pulsing with electric pre-game anticipation and jittery nerves.

The sprawling scene looked like something between a swap meet and the tailgate parties before a Chicago Bears game, a sheet-metal portrait of America itself. There were gleaming Caddies and Lincolns, and beat-up old trucks, late-model Benzes and Porsches, custom vans and motor homes. There was even an old Harley with a bag of clubs sticking out of the sidecar.

The lot made me think of those muddy, brawling Wild West towns that sprang up overnight around a saloon-brothel in the gold rush, and as I hunted out a space I felt more excited and alive than I had in years.

There is nothing elitist or exclusive about Q-School. Anyone with a birth certificate and three thousand dollars can tee it up. According to the entry form, you also need a letter from someone in "the golfing community" verifying that you know how to play, but what assistant pro is going to refuse to write a note for someone who has bought thousands of dollars of lessons from him or the head pro?

As a result, the range of skill and qualifications at Q-School is about as broad as any Sunday at your own course. That morning, there were golfers who had been on and off the PGA Tour for twenty years; there were former college stars and teaching pros and amateur state champions; and others who had never broken 90 honestly in their life.

As for myself, I am not officially even a scratch golfer. My lowest handicap, posted when I was nineteen and then again when I was forty-eight, was a 1.

While that may seem impressive to most golfers, it's diddly-squat on tour, where, if calculated on an average course, the actual handicap of a solid touring pro is a −3 or −4.

Statistically, of course, all but the very best of us were on a fool's mission — or in search of a miracle. We had no more likelihood of success than an old forty-niner panning for gold in a Montana stream. The golfers crowding the parking lot that morning weren't even there for the final stage of Q-School. This was just the regional qualifier.

The next day 240 golfers would play *one round*, with the top twenty-four spots getting added to the other 160 golfers who had already made it through regional tournaments held earlier in California and Texas.

Then those 184 golfers would shoot four rounds for exactly eight one-year spots on the Senior Tour.

With so many golfers and so few spots, the pressure was absolutely insane.

It was far worse than even the regular tour Q-School, where forty spots are up for grabs, and those who don't make it can consider the Nike, Asian, or satellite tours, and if all else fails, can at least look forward to Senior Tour Q-School down the road.

But for most of us, this was it. The last chance to dream. The final court of appeals.

Over the next five days, I got to witness the devastating effect that so much pressure can have on such delicate mechanisms as the golf swing and the human psyche.

Over the next four days, I saw and heard things on a golf course I hadn't experienced in four decades. It seemed that at any moment, half the field was muttering to themselves and pacing back and forth like expectant fathers in a maternity ward, and they were the ones with their shit together. Health nuts, who hadn't smoked in their lives, were inhaling two packs a day.

Playing in Q-School is like running a gauntlet. There are no winners, only a handful of scarred and bloody survivors.

Just thinking back on it gives me the yips.

Maybe it was because I didn't know any better that I found the pressure bracing rather than debilitating. Yeah, I was nervous and could barely sleep or keep down solid food, but never for a second did I second-guess my decision to try to qualify.

I was doing what I wanted to do. Finally. After all these years.

My streaking golf game seemed to have survived the trip intact, including my newfound and all-important ability to read the line on my putts. I was still playing the best golf of my life.

I shot a 67 in the qualifier to comfortably make it to the final stage, and when I opened with another solid 69, a local reporter wrote a story about a "jilted adman who may have saved his best lines for the Senior Tour."

Chapter 13

You know how some people are terrible to eat with? The food arrives and they attack it with such naked fear and longing that the sight of them makes you embarrassed to be a human being. It's the same with golf. Some people are fine to play with. Others exude such an ugly paranoia that just standing next to them can cost you three strokes a side.

And that's why in the early rounds of a tournament, particularly a tournament like Q-School, nothing is more crucial to your chances than the person you're paired with.

That's why I was lucky to be paired in the second round with a guy who introduced himself as Earl Fielder.

At five foot seven and 220 pounds, Fielder had the same brick shithouse physique as my grandfather when he was younger. According to a story I read in the local gazette, Earl Fielder was a retired army captain. After surviving four highly funky tours in Vietnam, he'd spent the last decade living in the woods outside Monroe, North Carolina, hunting, fishing, and overseeing his stock portfolio. Or, as he described it, "living off the fat of the land."

He'd also been honing his game. Although he didn't pick up a club until an R&R excursion to Thailand at twenty-five — "When I was a kid, the nearest public course that allowed black people on it was three hours away" — he had won the Carolina amateur three times in the past five years.

After a half-dozen holes I could see why. Earl Fielder could play the game. His swing may have been a little fast and short, but I had never seen anyone stand up to the ball so solid and strong. He looked as if he were rooted into the ground. And he was ridiculously straight off the tee, splitting the fairway drive after drive with a machinelike rhythm.

But it wasn't just his game that was solid. In the four-day freakathon that is Q-School, where even the most level-headed competitors are just a spike mark and a lipout away from a psychotic incident, Fielder was an oasis of serenity. After a three-putt on the second hole, for example, the other member of our threesome, a Venezuelan teaching pro named Hector Fernandez, had taken to crossing himself before every swing.

But Fielder actually seemed to have some kind of perspective on this whole affair. Before I had said a dozen words to him, I liked him, and felt nearly as comfortable around him as with my closest friends.

On the front side that day, Earl and I were steadily rolling along. We both made the turn at one under par.

But when we reached the tenth, a long, dangerous par 3 with water to the left, right, and behind the hole, there were already two threesomes backed up at the tee, which meant at least a fifteen-minute wait.

Under the circumstances, extra time to think is the last thing you want, but while Fernandez stood off to the side, flagellating himself in Spanish, and the other golfers squeezed in some last-minute work on their putting and chipping strokes, Earl just sat down — as if on a park bench — and lit up a long dark cigar.

"It's like an insane asylum out here," I said as I joined him.

"Yeah," said Fielder blowing out an aromatic stream, "after they cut back on the medication. It always pisses me off when people who don't know what they're talking about compare something to Vietnam, but in a weird way this really *does* remind me a little of Nam."

"I wouldn't know," I said.

"It's got the same spooky sunlit vibe, people tiptoeing on eggshells and squeezing their little good luck charms, hoping to God they won't fuck up and will somehow get through this thing."

"Sounds like the advertising agency where I used to work," I said. "Everyone walking around pretending they were invisible, hoping to survive another day. After twenty-three years they finally got me two weeks ago."

"Oh yeah, they ambushed your ass," said Earl.

"That's right," I said. "greased me right by the water cooler. So where do you stand in this thing?"

"One under," he said.

"Even," I said.

"So we're both still in the hunt."

Finally, the green opened up in front of us. Earl gingerly stubbed out his cigar, and after carefully wrapping it in tinfoil, returned it to his nylon club bag, which, like me, he was carrying himself.

"Earl," I said, "I'm going to find you Sunday when this thing is over. Buy you a beer."

"Looking forward to it, Travis."

Chapter 14

I was definitely still on the road to Lourdes. No miracles yet, but keep your mind open. Believe me, something strange and wonderful was going down here.

With Earl Fielder's example helping to steady my nerves, I shot my second straight 69. That put me at six under for the tournament and in ninth place overall.

I was so close to the Senior Tour, I could taste it, and figuring that playing safe wasn't going to get it done — the course was just playing too easy — on Saturday I came out blazing. I was firing for every flag.

On the front side, I put together my best run since my absentee Christmas dinner, going five under on the first eight holes. My swing felt solid, and I was seeing the line as if I were looking down the mahogany shaft of a pool cue.

By the time I teed it up on nine, I had already cashed in about one hundred feet worth of putts, including a forty-footer for eagle and three twenty-foot birdies.

The ninth hole at the Dunes is a tough par 4 with a blind tee shot over a rise, then a long second shot down to the green.

After hitting a respectable drive, I saw that my name had gone up on the leader board for the first time all week, not to mention, of course, for the first time in my life.

There I was, in third place, right behind Ed Sneed and Frank Conner. A big red McKinley. Followed by the denotation −11.

As I walked to my ball, I couldn't stop myself from savoring, if only for an illicit instant, the almost infinite satisfaction I would derive from informing friends and foes and doubters all, if I could somehow make it through to the tour.

With a downhill lie and 210 yards to the front edge, I pulled a 4-iron and caught it thin, but luckily came up short of the greenside bunker. With the flag tucked up tight just beyond the trap, I didn't have much green to work with, but if I could spin it close and sink a putt, I'd have a 31 for the front, and wouldn't have to perform any heroics coming in.

I took out my 60-degree wedge, and pictured a soft, lazy flop shot landing just on the front edge.

Don't get too cute with it, I told myself as I took a couple of long, loose practice swings, but as soon as I hit it, I knew that was exactly what I had done.

I didn't shank it or mishit it. I just hit it about two yards short, and it plopped as softly as an omelette into the far bank of the bunker, so softly that it didn't roll to the bottom, but stayed right where it landed — under the goddamned lip.

I couldn't believe my stupidity or, more accurately, I couldn't face it. I traveled in a nanosecond from an intimate little acceptance speech for three thousand, to stone-cold panic. Under the goddamned lip! Under the goddamned lip! UNDER THE GODDAMNED LIP!

At this point two very distinct voices lobbied desperately for sway over my stressed-out brain. One voice preached disaster control and begged for restraint. "Chip it backwards, take your five or your six, and get out of here in one piece. You're still young. You've got your whole life ahead of you."

The other voice was like a wounded beast, my own private Othello. It felt so betrayed and hurt by the last shot, so incredibly pissed off, it seemed bent on self-annihilation. It urged me to just wade in there up to my knees and gouge the ball out onto the green, like John Daly somehow did at 17 at the British Open.

I listened to the voice that was louder, the wounded would-be John Daly.

I marched down into the trap and aggressively worked my feet into the sand two feet below the ball.

When I had my balance and a firm picture of my shot in mind, I steeply lifted my wedge, but just as I brought it crashing down behind the ball, the quieter spurned voice of reason spat out a perfectly timed one-word character sketch: *"Asshole!"*

As a result, I neither blasted the ball out onto the green nor hit it backwards.

In fact, I didn't hit the ball at all, didn't come anywhere near hitting it, the forward blade of my wedge diving into the sand at least four inches behind the ball. Just close enough to bury it under a fresh layer of sand.

I felt as if I had just gotten out of my car in my driveway and discovered I had run over my dog.

A red-hot flush rose from my toes to my head, and wounded child-like eyes searched the scene for some kind of last-second loophole that would allow me to take the shot over.

Now I was lying *four*.

In a daze, I weakly chipped to the bottom of the trap — *five*.

And then to the very back of the green — *six*.

I knocked my first putt ten feet past — *seven*, rolled my second two feet short — *eight*, and tapped in for *nine*.

Nine! If an eight is a snowman, I had just shot an abominable snow-man, but what I had really done was shot myself in the foot, shot my-self right out of the tournament back to some even shittier job in some even shittier advertising agency. In one retarded spurt, I had pissed it all away, squandered my nest egg, taken all my birdies and my eagle and released them back into the sky.

Everything I had worked for all week had been undone in five minutes.

There was a coconut tree beside the green, and for a few scary seconds I seriously contemplated banging my head against the rough bent trunk until I was brain-dead.

Instead I did something, for which, in my own life, there is absolutely no precedent.

I forgave myself.

I said, Travis, you are a decent guy who loves his wife and his kids and his dog, and like everyone else on the planet has a God-given, inalienable right to fuck up.

It was as if the same two schizophrenic voices that did me in now put me back together. Or as if a third kinder, gentler voice had entered the conversation.

It was as if I had knelt down in a confessional booth and said, "Father, I have sinned. I shot a nine when the absolute worst I should have had was a five, which led me not only to utter God's name in vain but to consider the taking of my own life." And the kindly old priest, with the infinite compassion of the omniscient being he represents, had looked at me with sweet moist eyes and said, "It's a fucked-up world and game. Forget about it."

And I did.

I walked up to the tenth tee like a man who was happy to be six under for the tournament and happy to be alive. Then I went out and shot three under on the back side for my third straight 69. I had fallen back to sixteenth place, but I was still alive.

Dreams die hard. And sometimes they don't have to die at all.

Chapter 15

At 6:05 the next morning, I was awakened by such a clamorous ringing I thought the Winnetka High School marching band was practicing under my bed. In fact, it was my four alarm clocks.

Haunted by the story of a contending golfer who was disqualified after sleeping through his tee time on the final day of Q-School — arguably the most heartrending catastrophe in the history of sports — I had stopped at a drugstore after dinner and bought a second alarm clock.

Then halfway back to the Ben Franklin I said, "Why fuck around?" and bought two more.

It hardly mattered. When I got to the course, they were running an hour behind.

At Q-School the play is always painfully slow, but on Sunday the action virtually grinds to a halt. Players agonize over every club selection and every puff of wind, every break and every cut of grain.

In this overcooked atmosphere, watching someone card a bogey is like witnessing a violent mugging.

A double bogey is like a homicide.

Sunday isn't just achingly slow, it's also eerily quiet. There are no galleries, no applause, and no chatter among the players.

Even the birds stop chirping.

Despite the pressure, I can honestly say I had enjoyed my first three rounds. But Sunday was a death march.

I figured it would take 68 to finish in the top eight, and from the first drive, I was on my game. I was swinging well and seeing the line as clear as ever. But the damn putts just weren't dropping for me.

On the front side, I saw a dead center twelve-footer knocked off-line by a spike mark, watched an eight-footer do a 360-degree lipout, and another cling to the lip as impossibly as Cary Grant and Eva Marie Saint did on Mount Rushmore in *North by Northwest*. Sixty-eight was the number all right, but so far I wasn't even close.

The backside started the same way. One frustrating par after another. As I stepped up to the 15th tee, I was still only one under par, and running out of holes fast.

I needed — well, a miracle. I needed to go three under on the last four holes. I needed 68.

I got one of them right away on the short par-3 15th, when I hit a smooth 8-iron to fourteen feet and finally sunk a putt. Now, I absolutely needed birdie on 16, because 17, a 228-yard par 3 protected by trees on both sides, was an almost impossible birdie hole, a par 4 masquerading as a 3.

Sixteen, on the other hand, was a short, sharp dogleg right. It required a 4-iron, then a wedge to an elevated green. I hit my tee shot fine, but pulled my wedge, leaving me a very quick downhill thirty-footer, with a huge left-to-right break. For a right-hander like me, those are the hardest putts to read, but this time the line was crystal clear. I just hoped I could force myself to hit it hard enough.

In a silence so complete it recalled the void of nuclear disaster, I gave the ball a *ping* and watched it take off on-line.

For the first fifteen feet it was in. Then with rising horror I realized I had hit it way too hard.

I begged for it to at least catch part of the hole to slow it down.

It didn't.

I was now looking at a twenty-two-footer coming back.

I stood over the ball. I saw the line like the crease in a plebe's trousers. I knocked it in for par.

On to 17.

As I said, 17 was the hardest hole on the course, a hole that requires a perfectly faded 3-wood just to get the ball on the green. For the second shot in a row, I hit a pull. To get my birdie now, I was going to have to chip it in from the base of a tree.

The best I could do from there was five feet. Once again, I was lucky to crawl away with par.

What, you thought you were going to hear about the miracle on 17, a third of the way through the book? Get serious.

Chapter 16

Now I really was almost out of holes.

I had one left. And since 18 was a 560-yard par 5, I could still get to four under. *I just needed an eagle.*

Eighteen at the Dunes is a gorgeous finishing hole, long and straight, with the tee shot playing slightly downhill and the approach slightly uphill to a green backed by a white plantation-style clubhouse.

I hit my drive as well as I can — low and hard with a slight draw and it got all the way to the bottom of the hill almost 290 yards from the tee. But I still had another 270 left, this time uphill.

I mulled it over, but there was really nothing to think about it. An 8-degree driver is a tough-ass fairway wood, even with a flat lie, but it was my only chance to get there.

I took one long last look at the green, recalling how lovely and alluring it had seemed my first night in Tallahassee, and how I had walked over this very spot in the moonlight.

You're almost home, I thought to myself. Just give me one more solid swing . . . from the heels!

When you're trying to crush a fairway wood harder than you have any right to, there is a tendency to top it, and send a pathetic little dribbler about a hundred yards up the fairway. As I stood up to the ball, I told myself to squat down on that thing, and if anything catch it a little chubby. So as not to overswing ridiculously, I used a trick I've occasionally resorted to in somewhat less-pressured situations. Even though the flag hung straight down in the breezeless afternoon, I imagined a hurricane howling at my back.

All my little head games worked. Probably because I'm not that smart. I kept my balance and flushed it straight up the gut of the fairway, and after two low, hard bounces, my ball rolled onto the green. It was only the second time all week anyone had reached 18 in two.

I had just struck, back to back, two of the best 1-woods in my life, and hit them as straight as they can fly, but there was nothing triumphant about my walk up 18.

There wasn't a single spectator following our group or waiting on the green, and after six hours of fighting for my life I had one of the nastiest headaches I've ever hosted. I felt as if I were wearing a cap four sizes too small.

Eighteen feet stood between me and the Senior Tour. Eighteen feet between my shitty old self and my glorious future. Eighteen lousy feet.

Although I swore to myself I wouldn't stoop this low, it now seems almost eloquent. *So close and yet so far.*

Then again, as I looked over my putt, it looked closer than it did far. Considering where I was a month ago, eighteen feet looked pretty negotiable. Hell, it seemed like a gimme.

I was staring at a flat run across the grain, the kind of putt you have to hit crisply to keep on-line, but once again the line was clear. Just give it a good ride, I told myself, just give it a good ride.

Which I did . . .

Which I did . . .

Which I didn't.

I couldn't believe it. I had stood up to the most important putt of my life and left it two inches short of the tin. I will never say "Nice putt, Alice" to anyone again, if I live to be a thousand. Thank God, Joe and Chuck and Ron weren't there.

I tapped in for what seemed like the eighteenth time that day. A goddamn birdie! Then I slowly walked into the scorers' tent. I added and re-added my score, hoping that somehow I could get the arithmetic to spit out 68. But it kept coming up 69.

Finally I signed the card, then staggered back to a wall behind the green to watch the leaders finish up. So close and yet so far is about right.

Although I'd played pretty well, I felt neither satisfaction nor relief.

I wanted to call Sarah or Elizabeth or Simon and Noah, but I didn't have the strength. I was so tapped out, I almost fell asleep against the wall.

I actually heard the last threesome tee off a quarter of a mile away.

Ten minutes later none of them had appeared in the valley below the green. Strange.

In another five minutes or so, an electric murmur had begun to spread around the clubhouse.

I walked into the scorers' tent and heard a marshal ask into his two-way radio: "What the hell is going on down there, Orville? It's been twenty minutes."

A few seconds later, there was a crackle in the tiny speaker. It was followed by perhaps the sweetest piece of news I had ever heard: "*We got three golfers O.B.*"

For those unafflicted by this game, to be O.B. is to be out of bounds. As in deep gumbo.

On the final hole of the longest day, there had been the golfing equivalent of a three-car crackup on the last straightaway. All three players had hooked their drives onto Route 48 and out of bounds. By the time all the bodies had been cleared away and the paperwork filled out, 12 under par was good enough for eighth place.

I was a member in full standing of the PGA Senior Tour.

Chapter 17

I showered and changed, and dreamily wandered back outside. By now it was close to six, and the sun was dropping fast behind the huge wooden scoreboard that had been erected beside the 18th green.

It was that time in a Florida evening when the earth seems to catch its breath and sigh, and I felt as calm and quiet as the cool still air.

What I really felt was *different*. That who I was at that moment was a significantly different person from the one who had got up that morning and driven to the golf course, distinctly different from even the person who was in eleventh place less than an hour before.

I was more comfortable in my body. It was a place I wanted to be, a place I had been looking for for a long time, probably my whole life.

Although I'd managed not to dwell on it, and had done everything I could to keep the knowledge from overwhelming most of my days, I suddenly realized how depressed and ashamed of myself I had been for so long. What I had thought were just the usual regrets and doubts was actually a gorilla of self-loathing, and now, just like that, that hairy-handed gent had loosened his grip and slipped off into the Florida brush.

It wasn't that I thought I was better than anybody else, only that I was just as good. I felt I could stand alongside the next person and look him in the eye. Do you know what I mean? I felt I could *breathe*.

I walked to the base of the scoreboard, which loomed over the club-house lawn like a white version of that monolith at the start of *2001: A Space Odyssey*. I read down the names and scores painted in a lovely old-fashioned script until I reached my own, eight names down.

Travis McKinley.

Good God, I had really done it.

Golfers and their next of kin were still stumbling around the last green like dazed victims of a train wreck. No doubt about it, there were a lot more casualties than survivors on that final scoreboard. Maybe some day they would be able to recall with pride that they were even on the board at all, that they had not only come down to Tallahassee to chase their dream, but had performed well.

I doubted it. Some people say trying is all that matters, but unfortunately it's only the first step. Sometimes you've got to catch a break and win one, too. You've got to stand up on the bar and do the antler dance. Plus, as I now knew as well as anyone, people really suck at consoling themselves.

Chapter 18

"So tell me, Travis, what do you do for a living?" For twenty-three years, it was the question I dreaded more than any other. "What do you do?"

I work for an advertising agency. I'm an advertising copywriter. I write commercials.

God knows there are a lot worse jobs than being an advertising copywriter. And if that's what you want to do, be my guest. But for me, that unavoidable answer had been breaking my spirit for two and a half decades.

Now I couldn't wait for someone to ask me who and what I was.

"So tell me, Travis, what do you do?"

"I'm a professional golfer."

"No shit."

"Yup."

"You teach?"

"No, my friend, I learn. I'm a player. I'm a professional golfer on the Senior Tour."

There was a pay phone in the parking lot, and with a half-moon just appearing in the fragrant night, and my heart pounding in my chest, I made my call.

"Sarah," I said as soon as she answered the phone, "what am I?"

"What are you talking about?" she asked. "Are you calling from Florida?"

"What am I, Sarah?" I asked again, almost shouting the words. "What am I?"

The people milling around me were too caught up in their own miseries to find anything the slightest bit strange about my loud questioning, and perhaps, in her own way, so was Sarah. I had the terribly lonely realization that Sarah had no idea what I was talking about, and didn't even know exactly why I was calling.

"You're a lunatic," Sarah said with a familiar hint of a smile in her voice. "And I guess you're a decent father."

"I can't take the suspense any longer, Sarah, so I'm going to tell you what I am," I said, looking up at the forlorn moon. "I'm a professional golfer."

"You made it?" she said in amazement.

"I made it. I finished eighth. I have a spot in every senior tournament for a year."

"Congratulations," she said. "Listen, I'm really sorry to be telling you now. I really don't mean to spoil this, but I'm probably going to talk to a lawyer next week about a divorce."

For a few seconds I was too staggered to say a thing. You know that Dickensian crap about the best of times and the worst of times. I guess it's not crap.

"But, Sarah, we've barely even talked about this. Shouldn't we at least try to see someone?"

"You mean like a marriage counselor, Travis?"

"Yeah."

"You always end up with some Pollyanna on her second happy marriage."

I sighed. "It's just such a weird night, Sarah, and I don't even know what the point is if I can't share these little triumphs with you."

"This one isn't so little, Travis," Sarah said. "Save the charming modesty for someone else."

"You're right, it's pretty amazing. But don't decide now. Please. I'll be gone the next couple of months anyway."

"Not to change the subject, Travis, but there's a guy here who knows exactly how he feels about you, and he's been hanging around all day for your call. Let me get him."

I looked over my shoulder, where a line had formed behind me.

"Dad," said Simon, "you made it?"

"I finished eighth. I got the last spot. I'm a professional golfer," I said.

"You showed 'em, Dad," said Simon letting out a hoot. "You showed everybody."

"I really did, pal. Tell Noah for me, okay, and call Elizabeth."

"I can't wait to tell Pop," said Simon. "This is amazing."

"I got to go, Simon," I said. "There are all these people waiting to use the phone. I love you."

I had to get off so fast, not just because of the murmuring in the line behind me, but because as I thought of Simon and Noah and Elizabeth and Sarah and Pop, something just crumbled, and I started to cry. I don't mean some sniffles or a few tears of joy. I mean serious chest-heaving, with snot coming out of my nose, bawling that stood out even in this disaster area.

I cried for everything that had gone right and wrong for thirty years. I cried about Sarah. But most of all, I think I cried out of stunned gratitude. Despite my uncanny tendency to screw up, I had never given up on myself.

"Don't worry, pal," said a kind voice from the darkness, "you'll get it next year."

I sat down on the curb in the dark at the back of the parking lot, waiting for my crying jag to stop. It took a while, and I didn't care who saw me or what they thought.

Then I walked back to the clubhouse bar to go find Earl Fielder.

I owed him a beer.

Chapter 19

"You know the line 'This Bud's for you'?" I asked Earl, as I walked over to his table at the back of the bar and handed him one.

"I think I may have heard it maybe three times," said Earl, looking up from his *Barron's*. Earl had finished a very respectable thirty-fourth in the final standings. It wasn't good enough to make the tour, but he seemed his usual unflappable self.

"Well, I didn't write it," I said.

"No, I guess they wouldn't have fired you if you had."

"Anyway, cheers," I said. "I'm very sorry you didn't make it. You really helped me in the second round. More than you know."

"I'm glad you did make it, Travis. I really am," said Earl.

The 19th hole at the Tallahassee Dunes, a large restaurant-bar with a television at each end of the bar, was jammed and hopping every night all week, but that evening it was empty and subdued. Those who made it had the decency to celebrate elsewhere, and those who hadn't had tried to put as many miles between themselves and here as fast as possible.

But Earl sitting there with his long chocolate brown Habanas cigar and *Barron's* opened to the week's market analysis hardly looked like a man who had just missed qualifying by six strokes.

"What's your secret to sanity?" I asked. "I'd thought I'd find you muttering in your beer."

"I've been through too much shit to get bent about this," said Fielder matter-of-factly, "plus Microsoft went up eleven points this week. But what's with you? You look like a sponge."

"I called home," I said, "and the next thing I was bawling. It was like my father had come up out of the grave and told me he loved me."

"How come you never tried to play the regular tour?" asked Earl. "You got the game for it."

"In high school, it's all I ever thought about," I said. "Then I went to college and fell in love, and by the time I graduated I had a wife in medical school and a two-year-old daughter. Suddenly golf seemed irresponsible. Plus, I didn't learn how to putt until about three weeks ago. The irony of course is that the job I took instead proved not to be so safe either, and now my wife is probably going to file for divorce."

"Hold on," said Earl, savoring a long draw on his Cuban. "You just got fired. Your old lady's about to give you the boot, and you got all this unresolved shit with your old man. Next thing, you're going to tell me your dog has fleas."

"Ticks," I said.

"Travis, you're going to have me feeling sorry for you, and you're the one who made the goddamn tour," said Earl with a laugh. "Well, maybe you are kind of a mess, but you've got talent, and talent is rarer than you think."

"We'll find out soon enough."

"I tell you what," said Earl, "as I'm feeling so good about Microsoft, I'll make you a sweetheart deal. I'll caddy for you for six months, and you don't pay me anything but expenses and a commission on your winnings. It'll give me a chance to see what the big leagues are like, and in return I'll knock some sense into you."

"So you wouldn't be one of those read 'em the yardage and hand 'em the sticks kind of caddies?" I asked.

"Not a chance. With me you get the whole deal," said Earl. "Caddy, investment counselor, and sports psychologist. All or nothing."

I reached across the table and shook hands with my new partner.

Chapter 20

"Now on the first tee, from Winnetka, Illinois, Travis McKinley."

Thus spoke the starter at the FHP Health Care Classic in Ojai, California, and at 7:18 on a crisp Southern California February morning, with God, Dale Douglas, and Kermit Zarley as my witnesses, I officially began my Senior Tour career — by hooking my drive into the deep rough, and practically dancing down the fairway after it.

"Try to show a little dignity, for God's sake," said Earl, "you're not supposed to be thrilled with a hook into the bramble. You're embarrassing me."

"Anyone ever tell you you're cute when you're grouchy?" I asked.

"All the time," said Earl.

I tried to act cool, in a way vaguely befitting my newfound status as a member in good standing of the PGA Tour, but that's all it was. An act. If Q-School is the Inferno and Purgatory rolled into one, then the Senior Tour is Paradise. As designed by Robert Trent Jones, instead of Dante. And you don't even have to die to get there. You just have to get old.

Since Earl and I rolled into town on Wednesday morning, tournament sponsors had handed me the keys to a suite at the Marriott and a pearl white Lexus. I was assigned my own roped-off spot on the driving range furnished with a glistening mound of Titleists more pristine than I was used to *playing* with, let alone practicing with, and in case any of the paying spectators who wandered out to the range to pick up a thing or two from the pros couldn't quite place my swing, there was a large white placard with my name boldly printed on it, propped up in the grass just behind me.

Oh, and on my first day of practice, a rep from Calloway fitted me for a full-custom set of Big Berthas, from a 60-degree wedge to an enormous graphite-shafted, titanium-headed Great Big Bertha driver, with a sweet spot about the size of a frying pan.

And every time I turned a corner, I came face to face with another tanned mug from golf's Mount Rushmore. The King himself, Arnold Palmer, was hitting balls four spots down on the range. Isao Aoki parked his butt in the cubicle next to mine in the locker room. He turned out to be this incredibly suave, chain-smoking character, kind of like a Japanese Dean Martin. And one morning, when I charged a putt on the practice green, it smacked right into Lee Trevino's heel. "Sorry about that," I stammered, as embarrassed as a kid, "my name's Travis McKinley. It's a real pleasure to meet you."

"Travis McKinley," said Trevino with his enormous exploding smile, "glad to meet you, too. I read about you this morning in *USA Today*. Listen, don't worry about that 'Miracle of Q-School' crap. No one is going to admit it to you, but we're all miracles out here, every last one of us. Now go work on your putting, son. Based on that last stroke, you need it."

I just stood there with my mouth hanging open. Lee Trevino. Mex, who still wears a Band-Aid on his right forearm to cover an old tattoo, and in 1971 won both the British Open and the U.S. Open, and whose caddy Herman is more famous than half the guys on tour, and *he was reading an article about me?*

Beyond that, the guy was cool. And generous. And friendly. And despite being in his late fifties, he exuded more pure high-octane human juice than any person I had ever managed to stand next to.

He was right, too, about the frosty core of most of the players. When the Senior Tour was started, a lot was made about the unique camaraderie enjoyed by the competitors, and how that was such a refreshing change from the regular or "Junior Tour," as the seniors liked to call it.

Then the Senior Tour took off. The players started competing for a million dollars every weekend. And all that warm and fuzzy stuff flew right out the clubhouse window. The seniors may ham it up a little more than the regular Tour players, and have a more relaxed rapport with the galleries, but don't let that fool you.

These guys would rip out your heart and stomp all over it with golf spikes if they thought it would help them get another year on tour.

Actually, the Senior Tour reminded me of that old morning game show where they sent a delirious housewife into a grocery store, with only her greed and a shopping cart, and told her she could keep anything she could throw into it in sixty seconds.

As lucrative as the Senior Tour is, the clock is always ticking. Unless you're a superstar, you're lucky if you can hang on for four or five years before being pushed out by some spry fifty-year-old coming up from below.

But who cares? That first week, all those harsh realities were the furthest thing from my mind. I felt so carefree and unperturbable, I couldn't help but play well.

On a long course in tough, windy conditions, I shot 71, 72, 69 to tie for sixteenth and make my *second* nice check in two weeks.

Including the forty-five hundred I made for finishing eighth at Q-School (admittedly three thousand of that was my own money), I had now made twelve thousand four hundred in two weeks. Like shooting ducks, I thought to myself. Even Noah was impressed when I called home. In fact, it seemed everybody in Winnetka was pulling for me — except Sarah.

Chapter 2,

"I hope you've enjoyed your little tiptoe through the tulips, Travis," said Earl, "because the party's over."

"Excuse me?"

The two of us were sipping free beer in the lobby bar of the Marriott at the end of my first perfectly delightful week on tour, and Earl was already reading me the riot act.

"I don't know what *you* got in mind for the next nine months, but *I* didn't come out here to hump a bag for some starstruck tourist who can't tell the difference between a boondoggle and the chance of a lifetime. Travis, do you know how many golfers would kill their pets for a year's exemption? And the sad thing is, you could do some real damage out here. But you've got so much to learn it isn't even funny. So either you get serious, or I'm going back to Monroe and work on my own game."

I don't know if I was more embarrassed or grateful, because I knew Earl was right. In my twenty-three-year career as an advertising copywriter, I came up with all kinds of reasons why I was better off not trying particularly hard, and I still stand by most of them. But two weeks ago on a long hot Sunday in Tallahassee, all those reasons expired.

If I couldn't suck it up now, I was either a coward or a fool. And I didn't think I was either.

From that day on, I started eating, sleeping, and defecating golf. Not only did I play and practice eight hours a day, seven days a week, including at least four hours a day on the range and practice green, but I threw myself into it with a conviction and concentration I had never brought to anything else. For the first time in my adult life, I felt like I was laying it all on the line every day, putting my very soul into it, living like an artist.

One of my early projects, and something that most distinguishes a pro from a low handicapper, was distance control. When I first joined the tour, I was almost disappointed by the way the players struck the ball. The first time I saw Dave Stockton, I thought he looked like about a 5-handicapper. Then I saw him *putt*.

The fact is, even the hall of famers rarely hit it anywhere near dead-solid perfect. What the good pros do have, though, is this very keen bottom-line-no-bullshit understanding of their own ability, and that starts with knowing exactly how far they hit every club in their bag. Not how far they *wish* they hit it, or how far they hit it *once*, but how far they are going to hit it *under pressure* ninety-nine out of a hundred times.

After the tournament at Ojai, I set about trying to acquire and refine that same self-knowledge. The first month, I spent at least two hours a day working my way from my wedge to my 5-iron, until I knew within one or two yards how far I could expect to hit each one of them.

But, then again, I worked like a dog on every part of my game. One day I squeezed on some sunblock, grabbed a towel and a bottle of Gatorade, and spent an entire afternoon in a practice bunker. I know how long I was there because Trevino said hello to me on his way to a practice round, played the entire round, went into the clubhouse, showered, and had a sandwich, and when he came out I was still scooping little holes in the sand.

"If you're just trying to impress me, Travis," said Trevino, "it's working. Now, if you don't get out of there soon, someone's going to report you to the union."

I made a pleasant discovery. You work hard at something eight hours a day, you get better. Not a lot better necessarily, but a little better, and that's just fine, because improving at golf, or anything else probably, is just a matter of making an endless series of tiny improvements.

Slowly but surely, I began to feel like a professional golfer. I knew the exact distances I hit every one of my clubs. I didn't get uptight every time I had to lag a forty-footer or hit a flop shot out of the rough.

Obviously golf is not a craft that anyone ever masters, but one moment in my apprenticeship stands out.

It was in my fifth pro tournament, Bruno's Memorial in Birmingham, Alabama. Looking at a flyer lie in the rough, to a green that sloped sharply from front to rear, and a flag cut in the very front, I did something I had never even considered doing as an amateur. I hit the ball smack into the center of the greenside bunker. On purpose.

From there I blasted to four feet, and cleaned up my mess for par.

It was just a par, but it felt like a lot more than that.

Earl knew what it meant, too, because as we walked off the green, he stuck out his hand, looked me in the eye, and said, "Travis, welcome to the Senior Tour."

After playing the game for forty-two years, I felt like a serious golfer. No gimmes. No mulligans. No bullshit.

Chapter 22

Time for a golf quiz.

One question. Thirty seconds. Here goes.

You're in the second round of a tournament. You shot even par the first day, and come out on fire on Saturday, going four under in the first five holes. And let's say, for the sake of argument, that after a solid drive on the par-5 6th, you find yourself 205 yards from a small green, protected in front by water. Whatever little wind there is is from right to left.

What do you do? I'm asking, because in my sixth event, the Dallas Reunion Pro-Am, I found myself in this very situation. The clock has just started ticking. *What do you do?*

Do you go for the green and try to get to five or even six under par for the nine, or do you lay up and try to walk away quietly with your par? Remember, you're four under par. You're smoking. Do you keep the pedal to the metal and risk a crash, or do you ease off the gas until this nasty little stretch is safely behind you?

Tick. Tick. Tick. You're down to fifteen seconds.

So what will it be? The lady or the tiger? Greed or caution? The chump change in Bob Barker's sweaty fist, or what's behind the lovely high-heeled Carol and door number one? So what's it going to be, punk? Are you feeling lucky? Are you feeling talented?

There goes the buzzer. Time's up. Put your pencils down and pass your papers to the right.

You decided to lay up, didn't you? The more you mulled it over, the more it seemed like the only thing to do. After all, you thought, you're already four under for the nine, why push your luck.

I made the identical choice. So I'll tell you what happened.

Since I was only 140 yards from the start of the water, I hit a soft pitch to the water's edge. Then, wanting to make sure I wasn't going to get wet — I'm playing this hole conservatively, after all — I hit my second wedge a little strong and rolled it five feet off the back of the green. Then, after a so-so chip, I've got an eight-footer to save par.

I miss the putt and walk away not so quietly with a bogey.

By playing sensibly and intelligently, I had taken a possible eagle, or very likely a two-putt birdie, and turned it into a goddamn bogey, and completely blown my frame of mind.

You see, I had practiced and practiced and truly gotten to be a *better golfer*. Now, I had to learn to get used to the fact, or as the pros like to put it, I had to get "comfortable" with it.

I mean, why in the world, when the wind isn't a factor, would you not go for a green that's only 205 yards away, except for the fact that you've suddenly found yourself four under par and are starting to weird out and ask yourself all kinds of irrelevant questions?

"It's like you're embarrassed about being good, Travis," said Earl after the round. "Almost ashamed of it. And so as soon as you get three or four under, you start waiting for the golfing gods to turn around and punish your ass. Travis, it's no crime of nature for you to be good at something . . . particularly something as essentially meaningless as golf."

Plus, if I can wax philosophical for a paragraph, there's an even more fundamental principle involved here, and it applies to everything from what you decide to do for a living, to making an omelette, which is that there is nothing so consistently dangerous, not to mention more likely to mess with your head and leave you muttering into your beer, than playing it safe.

Of course, I could be wrong.

Chapter 23

When I look back on what took place at the BellSouth Classic in Nashville, Tennessee, on the first weekend of June, I can see now that Earl was dropping one hint after another about how it was going to end. But fortunately at the time, I was too caught up in the events myself to understand any of them.

For starters, there was Earl's slight, but detectable, limp. Maybe I wasn't looking closely enough, but in seven tournaments, I hadn't noticed Earl do that before.

Even more curious, however, was that Earl, who has never exhibited even the slightest tension on the golf course, and after a decade of being shot at in Southeast Asia considers the whole notion of athletic pressure insulting, was more nervous than I was.

Yes, I had just birdied three holes in a row and, yes, I was tied for the lead of a pro tournament for the first time. But still, it was only Saturday. The way I saw it, I should at least wait until Sunday to start choking my brains out.

And then there was Earl's *extreme urgency,* which seemed a little misplaced under the circumstances. Even after I had birdied 15, 16, and 17, Earl was still riding me like a jockey going to the whip in the homestretch. "We got to have one more birdie, Travis," said Earl as we approached the 18th green. "We just got to."

Now, I appreciate the value of a birdie as much as the next person, and I understand the need for working a hot hand for all you can get, but why, I wondered, was it so important right now?

And finally there was Earl's Cheshire cat grin when I did in fact sink that last ten-foot putt at 18 to take the outright lead, and the way he said under his breath, "Pebble Beach, here we come." Pebble Beach, America's most spectacular golf course, was going to be hosting the U.S. Senior Open a month later, but the only way I was going to get an engraved invitation to that dance was by *winning* a tournament before then, and despite my tiny one-stroke lead, this hardly seemed like a sure thing, or even close to it.

By that evening, all of Earl's nervousness had vanished, and throughout dinner he barely said a word. In fact, he was so uncharacteristically quiet, I finally had to ask him if he wasn't going to give me some kind of inspirational pep talk for the next day's round. "You know," I said, "something in the guru/sports psychologist vein."

"The way you're putting and swinging, Birdie Man," said Earl with a smile, "you could win this thing in your sleep."

"Oh well, then I'm not too worried," I said, "although I'm beginning to get a little worried about you."

"I know what you mean," said Earl, "I worry about myself every day. That's what keeps me sharp."

Despite being a tad mysterious, Earl's low-key behavior helped me relax. I had no trouble falling asleep, and once I did, I slept soundly.

Until three in the morning, when I was awakened by the cataclysmic sound of the sky being ripped open like a grocery bag. I stumbled out of bed and looked out the window. I couldn't see the terrace, it was raining so hard. And three and a half hours later, when I got up for good, it was still coming down in sheets.

I'm sure at this point, Ben Hogan would have scowled at the porous sky and demanded in no uncertain terms that it knock the shit off, so that he could go out and win his golf tournament without any damn meddling from on high. And no doubt, Jack Nicklaus would have viewed the prospect of getting his first pro win in anything less than regulation as equally repugnant.

But I'm not Ben Hogan, and I'm not Jack Nicklaus. I'm Travis McKinley. So if any of you had been in room 1215 at the Nashville Ramada that morning, you would have witnessed the highly undignified sight of a grown man in his baggy underwear falling to his knees on the motel broadloom and embarrassing God with half a dozen fervent prayers sprinkled piously with hallelujahs and amens, to keep that precipitation a-coming . . . "O mighty clouds," I'm ashamed to say I said, "please feel free to empty thyselves indefinitely upon these parched parts."

Five minutes later, my prayers were interrupted by Earl calling to extend his congratulations on my *first . . . pro . . . win*. Two hours later, I got the call from the tournament office. Would I please come over to the course and pick up my trophy and my check for $165,000.

Don't you just love this country?

I figured this was sufficient reason for waking up my heirs in Winnetka.

"One hundred sixty-five thousand dollars," said Simon groggily. "You know what that means?"

"What?" I asked.

"You're yuppie scum."

"Can't you just see me at the helm of a big burgundy Beemer?" I offered.

"Don't make me puke," said Simon. "Congratulations, though."

Where did my children acquire these embittered pinko values, I wondered. From me, I realized.

"You're not scum, Dad," said Noah, "you're just rich."

"Your daddy's rich and your mama's good-looking," I sang, bursting into Gershwin. "Can I talk to her?"

"She had to deliver a baby," said Noah. "You know Mom."

"And where is she delivering the baby to?" I asked, success having made me witty enough for your average four-year-old.

"Stop it, Dad," said Noah, who is definitely not average.

"You tell her for me, okay?" I said. "I'll call Elizabeth."

"Okay, Dad," said Noah. "I'll tell Mom."

After I called Elizabeth, Earl and I picked up the hardware and the software and headed directly to Nashville's most expensive nouvelle restaurant, where we behaved like any other pair of rich middle-aged friends addled by good fortune. We ate too much. We drank too much, and talked and laughed much too loud. It was wonderful.

Despite my windfall, it turns out I wasn't nearly as wealthy as Earl, who revealed for the first time that on a good day his stock portfolio was worth between one and one and a half million dollars. I still wrote him a check for $33,000.

Maybe it was the wine or the good company or both, but after a while I started to get emotional. "From now on, Earl," I said, "instead of calling me Travis, I think it would be best if you could just refer to me as the current champion of the BellSouth Classic."

"It would be my great honor," said Earl, who was clearly as moved as I was. "But that's quite a mouthful, don't you think? Particularly when you add the asterisk on account of it being a rain-win."

"Why don't you just kiss my asterisk," I said.

"Here's to the U.S. Senior Open," said Earl, lifting his champagne.

"To Pebble Beach," I said, meeting his glass. "I'm going to bring that course to its knees!"

"Oh, Jesus," groaned Earl. "May we not live to eat those words!"

If a bank had been open that late, we would have laughed all the way to it.

I tried to call Sarah when I got to the hotel, but she still wasn't back from the hospital, which left me feeling seriously unrequited. To cheer myself up, I went down to the front desk, made a copy of my $165,000 check, stuffed it in an envelope, and had it Federal Expressed to my old pal Mike Kidd in Chicago. Oh, and I added an incredibly catchy little slogan:

"Kiss my ass."

Chapter 24

"In all my years," proclaimed Earl, apropos of nothing, almost as if he were talking to himself or had suddenly decided to initiate a conversation with the setting sun, "I have never observed anything quite so sorry, so miserable, and downright pathetic as a human being in love."

After Nashville, the tour had headed to Phoenix for a week, and on our first evening in Arizona, I was sitting beside Earl on the terrace of the Hilton, wondering what Sarah was doing at that moment and where, if anywhere, I stood in her affections.

"Is that a fact?" I asked my spiritual and physical adviser.

"Let's take you, for example," he said.

"All right," I obliged. "Seeing as I'm not too busy at the moment."

"What do you see right now?" Earl asked.

"The sun going down, and the floor of the desert looking as if it's on fire," I answered.

"Would you say it's a pretty view, Travis?"

"Breathtaking, Earl."

"And how 'bout the weather? How would you describe that?"

"Pretty damn pleasant," I replied.

"Pleasant my ass," said Earl. "It's perfect. Christ, it's so perfect, I can't even feel the air on my skin. And what's that in your hand?"

"An ice-cold Budweiser. Can I get you one?"

"I'm fine, but thanks. How 'bout your bank account? How's that doing?"

"I don't mean to be crass, Earl, but it's six digits healthier than it was three days ago."

"Thank God for rain," said Earl.

"Crops got to grow," I agreed.

"And what is it exactly that you do for a living?"

"Earl, I play golf."

"Let me get this straight. You get paid — handsomely apparently — to play golf on the most beautiful courses in the country."

"It's the damnedest thing, isn't it?"

"So here you are nursing a cold one, taking in one of the more spectacular vistas on the planet, one hundred thirty-five gees accruing interest daily, following an improvement in your circumstances so extreme some might suspect God is playing favorites, and *how do you feel?*"

"Miserable," I said.

"I rest my motherfucking case. And yes, I will take that beer now."

Chapter 25

Four weeks to the day after my terrace chat with the duke of Earl, I stepped up to the first tee at the Nationwide Championship in Alfaretta, Georgia. I was a changed man.

How could it be otherwise? In a matter of months, I had shed my old life as an advertising copywriter and been reincarnated as a pro athlete. First, I made the Senior Tour. Then I won on it. I earned more money in two days than I had in two years. In the process, I had all but assured myself a second year on tour, earned an invitation to the U.S. Senior Open, and given myself a chance to vie not just for dollars but for a small piece of history.

Let me tell you the effect of all this fine fortune on my game and head.

I couldn't drive. I couldn't putt. I couldn't hit my irons. And I couldn't chip. If I left anything out, I couldn't do that, either.

In a month, I went from consistently breaking 70 to religiously topping 80. My previous three finishes were last, last, and last — *detect a pattern?* — and my scores at the Cadillac NFL Classic — 83, 86, 89 — may long live in infamy as the highest three-round total in the fourteen-year history of the Senior Tour. After my win in Nashville, I didn't suffer a letdown or a slump, I went into free fall.

My state of mind was about the same — a Molotov cocktail of depression and anxiety. If the yips is the nervous affliction that undermines the putting stroke, then I was suffering from a much more lethal and pervasive condition that sabotages every mental and bodily function. I started shaving with an electric razor for fear I would accidentally do myself serious harm.

All the most noted swing doctors paid house calls. David Leadbetter, acclaimed for his work with Nick Faldo and Nick Price, prescribed a complete overhaul by which I would come to make my torso and not my legs the "engine" of my swing. Butch Harmon squinted at me on the range. Jim McLean analyzed every millimeter of my swing on videotape. And the Irish mystic Mac O'Grady gave me a two-syllable mantra to repeat at the top of my backswing. I'd tell you what it is, but I paid two thousand dollars for it.

Every day I began to feel more and more like the label I had been given in that article Trevino had referred to — "the Miracle of Q-School." A sham. This year's impostor. A party crasher. I thought I might become the first professional golfer to ever leave the tour — out of embarrassment.

No doubt I was mentally exhausted and overgolfed. Try playing golf forty-five days in a row, after playing twice a week for thirty years. But more than anything else, I was homesick. I missed my family. I missed Noah and Simon and Elizabeth. I missed Pop and my tick-infested pooch. And I missed Sarah more than I ever had in my life, because, by this cruel twist of fate, I seemed to have lost her just as I'd found something to share with her.

Yet as much as I had wanted to go home, I had also been dreading it, because I feared that the only thing Sarah had to give me was even more conclusive bad news.

What if after thinking it over quietly and objectively for a few weeks, she had come to the inescapable conclusion that she was better off without me? If that was her decision, I wasn't sure I would ever recover from it. On the other hand, my fears were so bad, reality couldn't be any worse.

It was time to talk to Sarah, no matter what she had to say. It was more than time to hug my kids. It was time to go home, even if in some way it turned out to be for the last time.

Chapter 26

On Monday morning, as I drove my rental car out of the airport, from O'Hare to Winnetka, there was no giddy sense of excitement and anticipation.

There was no Sinatra in the tape player singing "Come Fly with Me." There was only silence and dread.

Sometime that evening I was going to have what might end up being my last genuine conversation with Sarah, and that possibility was too awful to consider, let alone accept.

As I pulled onto my street, Old North Winnetka Road, I felt like a fifty-year-old Adam, sadly looking over his old neighborhood one last time. Every familiar detail, from the circular driveway on the Lampke house to the speed bump in front of the Crasswellers', felt like something I was about to lose.

When I called Saturday night and told Sarah I was coming home for a visit, she was hardly enthusiastic. She had to work Monday, she said, and wouldn't be back till late — but Elizabeth, who was visiting for the weekend, immediately decided to stay a couple of extra days. And Simon and Noah announced that they'd gladly skip their soccer practice and day camp.

Nevertheless, on my flight and drive home, I thought mainly of Sarah. I can't explain why, unless it was because I had come to feel as undeserving of the kids as of Sarah, but I didn't believe that my children were going to miss me that much. Like a lot of fathers, I had begun to see myself as the family's one weak and dispensable link. I half-expected to walk in my door and find every trace of me removed from the shelves.

Instead I found Simon, Noah, and Elizabeth waiting in the front yard, holding a sheet with painted letters reading "Home of Travis McKinley, BellSouth Classic Champion!!!"

Man, what a cool sight that was. And when I stepped out of the car, Noah jumped into my arms and wrapped himself so tightly around my neck, I could barely breathe. Even Simon and Elizabeth hugged me in a way they never had before.

But it wasn't just the physical wave of affection. It was the way they looked at me. They were trying to make something so goddamn clear that even a fool like myself couldn't misread it, or turn it inside out. *They loved me. They missed me. They were proud of me.*

I was proud of what I had accomplished, too, but lately I'd been so desperate about Sarah, it had lost a lot of its meaning. But to them, this whole thing had been a pure kick and more. "Dad, I always told my friends you were this stud athlete," said Simon, "but no one believed me. Now it's not up to them whether they want to buy it or not."

Even Elizabeth was gushing. "I swear to God," she said, "you're the hero of the entire faculty of the Yale Medical School. You'd think you'd won the Nobel Prize for medicine the way the head of the department treats me now. In fact, that would be a big step down in his eyes. Maybe it's because they all play golf, and they suck, but all they do is ask about you."

"You're cool, Dad," said Noah into my neck. He had still barely loosened his grip, and in two days would let me put him down for a total of ten minutes.

That day was one of the best of my life. It made me realize that no matter what happened, I wasn't going to lose them. It was also a revelation. I'd never understood how desperately kids want to feel proud of their father. It made me think my little run could have a bigger impact on them than me, by letting them know it's all right to do what they want. They don't have to resign themselves to some soul-destroying nine-to-five they hate. There are possibilities. I know they've learned some of this from Sarah already, but they had to see it from me, too. It's hard to explain.

I don't know how aware they were of the troubles between Sarah and me. Elizabeth and Simon must have known about them. Maybe they all did, because the push for us to do some kind of family activity came as much from them as me.

That's how we ended up going swimming at the gorge, one of those perfect anonymous little swimming holes at the end of a country road on the very outskirts of town, where I'd taken Elizabeth and Simon at least once every summer, and which had assumed a mythological status in the big bright dome of Noah's.

We got to the gorge at three on a perfect July afternoon, and for about two hours we had it completely to ourselves.

The water was chilly and quick, but the sun on our backs, as we sat on the half-submerged boulders strewn across the thirty-foot-wide stream, was strong enough to keep us from getting too cold.

Simon, wearing his beloved Oakley shades and the light bouncing off his earrings, crouched on a stone the farthest out.

A couple yards away perched Elizabeth, like some brainy Ivy League mermaid, her beautiful brown hair pulled straight down her narrow back.

Noah sat on my lap in his life preserver, on a wide stone ten feet from the shore. For one memorable stretch, we just smiled at one another, and no one said a word, the only sound water rushing over flat stones.

Chapter 27

"So how's that baby doing?" I asked Sarah. She had just arrived home from the hospital. I was waiting nervously in the kitchen.

"Which one?" asked Sarah, only meeting my gaze for a second. She dropped her things on a chair and poured herself a glass from the half-empty bottle of white wine in the refrigerator.

"The first baby born in Winnetka this year," I said, "the New Year's baby."

"Oh, she's doing fine," said Sarah. "She's got this tiny pierced nose. She's Indian."

Noah had finally passed out at 10:00 P.M., Elizabeth and Simon at about 12:30, but Sarah didn't arrive home until almost two in the morning. Although it was possible some hospital emergency had kept her that late, it seemed more likely that she had stayed at work so long because she was dreading this conversation as much as I was.

At some point close to a year ago, Sarah had mostly stopped talking to me. In the beginning she insisted that nothing was the matter, then eventually conceded there was. And now in the past couple of months, she was talking about the possibility of a divorce. All without really telling me why.

Eventually, I had no choice but to conclude that the reason Sarah had no interest in talking was that, in her mind, it was already over.

"Why does this have to happen, Sarah?" I asked her now.

"I don't know, Travis. I've asked myself the same question."

"Well, when did it happen?"

"Travis . . ." She began to say something, then looked down at the counter and started to cry.

"I've changed," I said. "I couldn't change before, working at Burnett. I didn't even understand why. All I knew was that it felt all wrong."

"Oh come on, Travis."

"Sarah, I know I've been a drag for a while. I know I let you down sometimes."

"After we had Noah, and even that didn't cheer you up, I figured we never meant that much to you all along."

"Sarah, until that night I got through Qualifying School, I didn't know myself how unhappy I was. But it's not because I didn't love you and the kids. I'm sure I seemed like this ungrateful wretch, but unfortunately having a great wife and wonderful children doesn't make you love yourself any more. It just makes you love them."

"It's too late," she said. "I'm really sorry. Anyway, I'm not sure I would know what to do with this new Travis. Maybe I'm setting you free."

"Sarah, I don't want to be free. I want a ball and chain, and a pick-proof lock."

"You've always had such a romantic notion of marriage, Travis," said Sarah, half smiling through her tears.

"Sarah, you're it for me," I pleaded. "You always have been. I don't know what I'll do if I can't watch you get old and wrinkled."

"I'm already old and wrinkled."

"Like hell you are," I said. "I want to be able to look over at you and remind you how beautiful you are, knowing I've been through the whole thing with you."

"You don't always get what you want, Travis."

"Can't we try something, Sarah?"

"It's just too late, Travis," she said. "I wish it wasn't. I really do."

And then Sarah went up to bed alone.

Chapter 28

Later that morning, my ninety-three-year-old grandfather — he had celebrated his birthday two weeks before by shooting a tidy 98 — stood in the middle of the 12th fairway of the Creekview Country Club and dropped three Titleists onto the rich, green sod.

There may be nothing much worse than a Chicago winter, but there's nothing much better than a Chicago July, and that morning was a fine example of the species, with the temperature in the low eighties and just enough breeze to keep the air on its toes.

So much had changed since I'd been here before, and perhaps to remind me of that fact, Pop had walked me out to the very same spot we had visited on our last playing lesson. The fairway that had been hard and muddy back then was now covered with thick, luscious grass. The huge oak some forty yards away, which had served as a leafless obstacle, was now full and green and shimmering.

"Pop," I said, "Sarah wants a divorce."

"Well, Travis, what do you want?" he asked, as if I still had a choice in the matter.

"I want us to stay together."

"You tell her that?"

"Yup."

"You've done about all you can, then. How love gets doled out is one of the great mysteries of the planet, but one thing I've learned is that you can't force someone to love you. It's a little bit like chasing birdies. Wanting them too much only makes it worse."

"Pop, I'm feeling like a fraud out there on the tour," I confessed.

"Travis, where does this come from, this picking at everything until you find the tin under the gold? There's nothing fake about you, Travis. If anything, you're too goddamn real for your own good."

"So what do you want me to hit, Pop?" I finally asked, looking down at the three balls he'd dropped.

"I don't want you to hit anything, Travis," he said, his eyes sparkling with a light that remains utterly impervious to his years. "As far as I'm concerned, you've got nothing left to prove to me or Sarah or your father or anybody fucking else. All I want you to do is pick up those balls, and play with them at the Open next week, and I want you to enjoy yourself for Christ's sake, because I'll tell you one thing, I'm going to enjoy watching you. And by the way, Travis, there isn't a goddamn thing wrong with your swing."

"Pop, you haven't even seen me hit a ball."

"I don't have to." And with that, Pop turned and headed to the clubhouse. "The lesson's over, Travis," he said. "Let's go have a drink."

Chapter 29

Three hours later, I was standing at the corner of Commonwealth and Baxter in Chicago, my hands trembling like an old rummy, and a ridiculous smile plastered across my face.

Although the evidence was overwhelming, I could still barely believe what I had just done.

As always, my visit with Pop had greatly improved my frame of mind, but as hard as he'd tried, he had not come close to steering my mind away from Sarah. And on my way back to O'Hare to catch a flight to San Francisco for the U.S. Senior Open, I made a slight detour, and did something that under the circumstances might reasonably be interpreted as legally insane.

And yet for some reason, as I stood on the sidewalk in the lovely afternoon sunshine, elegant shoppers trotting briskly past me in their designer dresses and suits, I had no desire to undo it. In fact, what I had done was so over-the-top that it gave me a kind of peace of mind that comes from knowing you've done about all you can. After all, as both Pop and Sarah had pointed out, "not everything is up to me."

So what exactly had I gone and done that left me feeling so out of my element on that Chicago street corner that I might as well have been naked?

I'd like to tell you. I truly would. But I just can't.

It's too embarrassing.

Part 3

Miracle on the 17th

Chapter 30

The full, otherworldly, music-of-the-spheres significance of being at Pebble Beach and playing in the U.S. Senior Open didn't sink in until moments before the first round on Thursday.

That was when Earl slid up behind me on the mother of all practice greens, slapped me on the shoulder, and said, "Travis, let's go to work."

Till then, I had been distractedly lagging forty-footers across the huge lightning-fast ellipse, as mesmerized as any tourist by the rugged coastal grandeur of the place, and the brilliant godlike Northern California light that gave every surface a metallic sheen.

Now, as we worked our way through the crowd, my legs forgot how to walk, and as I frantically tried to remaster the basic right-foot, left-foot concept, I thought of James Cagney being led on that long last walk from the Big House to the gas chamber in *Angels with Dirty Faces*.

I'd only been more nervous on a golf course once. That was the afternoon, forty-two summers before, when after three years of beating balls, my grandfather finally decided I could play an actual round, and took me to Hubbard Heights, the more threadbare of Winnetka's two public courses.

At the Heights, the first tee is set up alongside a large Italian restaurant-bar that the blue-collar regulars have turned into their own country club, as exclusive in its own way as Augusta National, and that afternoon the large concrete terrace was filled with a rowdy crowd of plumbers and carpenters that suddenly quieted as I stepped up to my first real golf shot. I took a shallow breath and poured my cut-down driver straight as a die 140 yards up the rocky fairway, eliciting appreciative hoots and whistles from the peanut gallery, and a warm "I guess you're ready" from my grandfather.

I guess I could have used Pop's soothing influence once again, because on my first official drive at Pebble Beach, all I could muster was a weak push that left me in the first cut of rough, 185 yards from the green. But I was just as thrilled with it as with that first drive at Hubbard Heights.

My playing partners the first two days were Jim Colbert and South Africaner Simon Hobday. Colbert, who has never been out of the top five on the Senior Tour money list, is a granite-jawed, flat-topped, ex−football player, whose on-course demeanor falls somewhere between chilly and downright grumpy. Hobday, who wears a huge black Crocodile Dundee hat and a Yosemite Sam mustache, is warm and outgoing. But they both play Big Guy macho golf.

"Look at those two crackers strutting up the fairway," said Earl, "they think their balls are made out of brass." I know it's not the fault of Colbert and Hobday that they happen to have been brought into this world big, beefy, and bouncy, but as someone who at six two has never weighed in at more than 151 pounds, I've always competed my hardest against wide-bodies. As Earl suggested, I went to work.

The Open is one of only four Senior events that have a halfway cut, so the pressure is on from the first hole. At the start of the week, my only goal was to play all four days. "Pars will do just fine," Earl kept reminding me, and although I was all over the place with my driver and irons, I just kept grinding away.

All the hours I'd been putting into my short game were starting to pay off. I missed ten greens, but I got up and down on eight of them. Offsetting the two bogeys with one birdie gave me a one-over-par 73. That was one better than Colbert, one worse than Hobday, and right about the middle of the field.

The best news of the first day was my putting. I was seeing the line again, and it helped me sink a handful of nasty six-footers to save par.

After the round, I went to the range and tried to straighten out a tee-ball, whose unguided flights had taken me to some of the least scenic parts of America's most scenic golf course.

"I can't believe people are actually going to stand and watch me hit balls," I told Earl as a large crowd began to form behind me.

"Don't worry, Hogan, they're not here for you," Earl quickly informed me.

I looked over Earl's shoulder and saw Herman, Lee Trevino's enormous caddy, setting up shop in the spot next door, and then Mex himself, his huge grin bursting his tanned, leathery face into long straight lines.

"How you hitting 'em Travis?" Trevino asked.

"Not too bad, Mr. Trevino," I said.

"Cut the crap, McKinley," said Trevino with a cackle. "If he's so goddamn respectful," Trevino asked the crowd, "why's he trying to take food out of my kids' mouths?"

By now the sun was going down and the range was filling with warm, golden light. Although I was worried about why I couldn't hit the ball straight, and if I would still be seeing the line tomorrow, and if I'd ever be seeing Sarah again on a regular basis, I was suddenly overcome with a sense of well-being I hadn't felt since I was a kid.

To put it simply, I felt happy. Whole.

Hitting balls on my left was Hiroshi Ishi, a really fine Japanese player from a little fishing village outside Tokyo, who barely speaks a word of English. On my right was the legendary Trevino, a former driving-range hustler who has won seven majors and untold millions.

But on that beautiful late afternoon our vast differences seemed beside the point. We were all doing exactly what we wanted to do, exactly where we wanted to do it. We were professional golfers and immensely proud of it.

Chapter 31

The Senior damn Open at Pebble Beach.

Friday was a slightly tenser, more nerve-racking version of Thursday. Kind of like a bicycle tire with ten pounds more air in it. I hit a few more greens, sunk a couple more putts, and shot a one-under par 71. That got me through to the weekend, six strokes behind leader Bob Eastwood. I wasn't tearing it up, or doing anything even remotely miraculous, but I had survived the cut.

It was on Saturday, another perfect California morning, that I made my move.

The strange happenings began on the par-4 3rd hole, when I got a little too jacked up on the tee and snap-hooked my drive into the deep, gnarly U.S. Open rough.

Three shaky shots later, I was looking over a circus sixty-footer with more breaks, dips, and rises between me and the hole than between me and Sarah, and as I stood over the ball, I was just hoping to somehow two-putt and escape with my mental health. Dialing in about sixteen feet of break, I sent the ball on its way, and after what seemed like about ten minutes the ball slid into the back of the hole, like a dog that had found its way home. "Now that's what I call a world-class five," said Earl.

With the near disaster behind me, my round turned as if on a hinge. From that point on, I felt so incredibly serene and quiet inside, it was as if I were sleepwalking, or standing outside myself altogether. Either that or someone had spiked my Gatorade with Prozac.

I didn't make another bad swing all day. I didn't have another negative thought. I was in every fairway, on every green, and hitting my irons so stiff I was looking over makable birdie putts on every hole.

With a clear white line once again showing the way, I rolled in nine of them, five on the front, four on the back, for an eight-under-par 64.

Jim Colbert passed me near the scorers' table and didn't say a word.

And so that evening as Earl and I sat quietly in my hotel room, me nursing a beer and trying to reread a two-month-old airline magazine, and Earl smoking one of his beloved Cubans and perusing the *Wall Street Journal*, I was the sole leader of the U.S. Senior Open.

Tied for second two strokes back, were a couple of fellows you might have heard of — Raymond Floyd and Jack Nicklaus.

Chapter 32

Earl and I spent Saturday night trying not to freak out. We couldn't watch television because I was on every channel, and it was hard to do much else, because the phone never stopped ringing.

First it was ABC, CBS, and NBC. Then CNN, ESPN, and the Golf Network. I even got a call from Radio Free Europe, but the one call I wanted, from Sarah and the kids, never came, and every time I called home all I got was that coldblooded answering machine.

As far as my interviews went, I pretty much told them all the same thing. "I'm not insane yet," I said. "I know there's no reason to expect I can hold off two of the best golfers to ever play the game on one of the hardest golf courses in the world in the final round of a major. I just don't want to embarrass myself in front of fifteen million people."

After about six of these sound bites, Earl couldn't take it anymore.

"I hope you don't really believe all that modest politically correct bull-shit you've been serving up for mass consumption," he said. "You shot a sixty-four today, and now you're going to roll over?"

Earl finally unplugged the phone and was about to leave me to my anxiety when there was a light knock on the door.

"Who the hell is it now," Earl snorted to himself, "Bill and Hillary?"

Actually, it was Lee Trevino, looking all decked out and kind of weird in a jacket and tie, apparently just having got back from some corporate function.

"Mr. McKinley, I don't know if you remember me," said Trevino, "but I was practicing next to you on the range the other day."

"I deserve this," I said.

"I can't stay, and I know you got to get some bad sleep," said Trevino, "but I just wanted to wish you guys good luck tomorrow. Remember, there's a reason you're leading this tournament by two strokes, and it's not luck. You've worked as hard on your game as anyone out here."

"Thanks a lot," I said, "no matter what happens."

"And one other goddamn thing," said Trevino.

"What's that?"

"Call me Lee."

Chapter 33

July twenty-first.

Early Sunday afternoon, about twenty to two.

Pebble Beach.

The last threesome of the U.S. Senior Open.

Raymond Floyd. Jack Nicklaus. And yours truly, Travis McKinley. This is as about as real as it gets.

Or should I say unreal.

Brent Musberger and Peter Alliss were in the tower. The Kodak blimp was lazily circling overhead, and if I'm not mistaken the man leaning over the ropes strung tight around the first tee, wearing a tartan kilt, a tam-o'-shanter, and a "Travis Rules" T-shirt was Bill Murray.

And waiting ominously like a video angel of death about half-way down the side of the first fairway was Bob Rosburg, the former

PGA champion, who would be tracking us for the entire eighteen holes.

For those who don't squander vast amounts of their leisuretime on TV golf, Rosburg, called "Rosi" by his colleagues in the booth, is famous for pumping up the drama of even the most boring finish by mournfully whispering, "*Oh, he's just dead!*" about any shot that rolls even slightly astray.

I was just taking a few last freaked-out practice swings and trying not to hyperventilate when Earl snorted, then sighed, "Oh shit."

I turned around and saw what he was reacting to. There standing at the front of the ropes, having flown in from Chicago that morning, was the entire surviving population of Winnetka McKinleys, from Pop to Sarah to Elizabeth to Simon and Noah. It was a sight so welcome I thought for a second it was a mirage.

"It was his idea," said Elizabeth, lifting up a blushing Noah. "He threatened to go on a hunger strike if we didn't come."

They had arrived with so little time to spare I barely had time to kiss and hug my way down the line before nervous officials were calling and waving me to the tee.

"Isn't this great?" I said to Earl as we headed back to the center of the tee.

"Wonderful," said Earl with disgust, as he handed me a driver. "What's the matter, your dog doesn't like to fly? I'm just going to say one thing and then we're going to move on. This is not a family reunion. This the final damn round of the U.S. Open."

Just to let Earl know I had everything under control, I stepped up to my drive — as the overnight leader I had honors — and, as if I were alone on the range, blistered my first drive down the center of the fairway.

"You're The Man!" shouted Murray as my ball rocketed off the face of my driver. "And there are not a lot of us left."

Chapter 34

The next three hours or so were the most exhilarating of my life. They were also the most excruciating and heartbreaking.

For eighteen holes, I didn't take a relaxed breath. I didn't step up to a single tee shot that I wasn't afraid I might shank, or pull back my putter without the fear of a stub. I had no business being out there in the final threesome with two of the greatest golfers to ever play the game, and all of us knew it. I was in so far over my head I should have been carrying a periscope.

To keep me from being utterly overwhelmed by my surroundings and opponents, Earl had decided the night before that, after a quick handshake on the first tee, I wouldn't make eye contact or talk to either Nicklaus or Floyd the rest of the round. "We're not out here to relish the experience, or so thirty years from now you can plop your great-grandchildren on your arthritic knee and tell them that one Sunday you went head-to-head with the Golden Bear and the Great Raymondo. We're here to win. Just like them."

Whatever you say, Earl. And Earl was right about them trying to intimidate me. In fact, on the very first tee, Floyd, in an obvious gibe at my one soggy triumph, turned to me and said, "Doesn't look like rain today, Travis. Not a cloud in the sky."

"It's a good thing," Earl answered for me, "because I didn't even pack a rainsuit."

My biggest problem was my oldest problem, the putter. Under the extreme pressure, my ability to read the line was coming and going on every other hole. On some I saw the line with dazzling clarity. On others the green was *swimming* at my feet. Some holes, I rolled the ball like Crenshaw, knocking in field-goal-length putts. On others, I putted like a 14-handicapper choking his brains out over a four-footer that decides who pays for the hot dogs at the turn.

Ironically, the result of all this Sturm und Drang was about the same as a steady succession of pars. An unexpected benefit was that my personal emotional roller coaster was distracting to Nicklaus and Floyd.

I may have been throwing up on myself every couple of holes, but I refused to go away. And as we stood on the 17th tee, I was, as Musberger informed viewers in the dramatic stage whisper reserved for such occasions (I've since watched the telecast on tape a couple, three times) "still very much in the hunt."

I was one over par for the day, five under for the tournament, and *one behind* Nicklaus and Floyd, who were tied for the lead.

If anyone's interested, here's my scorecard through the first sixteen holes:

Par	4 5 4 4 3 5 3 4 4 36	4 4 3 4 5 4 4 3 5 36
Nicklaus	4 5 3 4 3 5 4 4 4 36	4 3 3 4 4 4 4
McKinley	5 4 5 3 4 3 5 5 4 38	3 4 4 3 4 4 5
Floyd	4 4 4 4 3 4 4 4 4 35	4 3 3 4 5 4 4

Chapter 35

Ah, sweet 17. Perhaps you never thought we'd get here. I know I had my doubts.

The 17th at Pebble Beach is a 209-yard par 3 that runs perpendicular to the coastline, with the green tucked up right against the Pacific and framed by a cypress as ancient and solitary as the Joshua tree.

Not only is the green extremely small and severely sloped, but the hole is constantly buffeted by the strong ocean winds. Depending on which way the wind is blowing, the hole can require anything from a 7-iron to a driver.

On Sunday, Jack and Raymond pulled out 2-irons, striking them so cleanly they had the high parabolic trajectory of 5-irons before they landed softly on the distant green.

Under the circumstances, hitting 2-iron was a little rich for my blood, so I tried to cut a high soft 3-wood. I caught it flush and watched it hang over the Pacific — then lazily drop out of the sky, landing, as Sam Snead used to say, like a butterfly with sore feet.

The ball nestled nine feet from the cup. The crowd at the green whistled and cheered.

After Raymond and Jack graciously missed their birdies and collected their automatic pars, I looked over my putt to tie.

For a second, as I crouched behind the hole and squinted at my ball, I had the hugely unsettling feeling of *not knowing exactly where I was*.

Was I at Pebble Beach in the final round of the U.S. Senior Open, or right back where I had started six months before on Christmas Day, standing on another 17th green, looking over a nine-foot putt that would change my life?

The two putts even had the same break — right to left — and speed — fast — and once again I could see the line as clearly as if I had snapped it with a chalky carpenter's string.

But there was a difference. This time, standing on the far side of the green on the exact line of my putt was Sarah, and with her dark-brown hair and sparkling eyes she looked at least as beautiful and determined and animated as the day we met. Based on what I did next — it occurs to me now — maybe I wasn't seeing the line of my putt at all, but only the line of my heart.

"Travis," I heard Earl whisper nervously behind me, "you all right, Travis?"

"All right?" I thought to myself, "of course I'm not all right."

I slowly walked back to the other side of the hole, but instead of stopping at my ball, I kept going until I had left the green altogether and was standing beside Sarah on the front edge of the murmuring gallery.

At that point, Sarah, along with about fifteen million other people, including the TV announcers Musberger, Nantz, and Rosburg, my grandfather, my playing partners, my children, and most of all Earl, concluded that I had finally fried my circuits and lost it altogether.

In a way, they were right. I had lost it.

But I didn't lose it that afternoon. I lost it thirty-one years before on a spring morning at the University of Chicago when I saw Sarah standing off by herself before a biology lecture. I lost it again when I saw Sarah fixing her hair in the mirror, minutes before we got married in her parents' backyard on a perfect June day. And I lost it beyond any hope of ever getting it back when I saw her holding day-old Elizabeth in the hospital the morning after Elizabeth was born.

In one way or another, I think I've lost it every time I've looked at her or talked to her, and if there is anything I can do about it, I am determined to stay lost until that chilly winter morning when I close my eyes and heart for the last time.

"Sarah," I whispered, "I bought this the week I came home to Winnetka, and I'm afraid if I carry it around with me for another second something very bad is going to happen to my heart."

I held out a diamond ring, just like the one she had lost on our honeymoon.

Actually, it was slightly nicer. All right, it was a lot nicer.

After leaving Winnetka last week, I didn't drive directly to the airport. I had stopped first at Harry Winston's, Chicago's most pretentious and overpriced jewelry store, and for some reason I can't logically explain, I kept asking the salesman to show me something a little bigger, more dramatic, and more radiant, until he showed me the ring I had just showed Sarah.

As you might suspect, size, drama, and radiance are not something they give away at Harry's. As a matter of fact, they put a certain premium on it. Fortunately, however, you can still get a rather lovely stone and setting for $135,000.

That's not a typo. I spent my entire BellSouth winnings on the ring. I mean what the hell. It was a rain-shortened win. I didn't deserve it.

But Sarah did.

As I stood there on the outer edges of the 17th green, I was shaking a little. I looked into Sarah's eyes and I was close to losing it.

"I love you, Sarah," I said, and to my everlasting amazement and happiness and infinite relief, she let me slide the ring gently on her finger. "I shouldn't, Travis, but I love you, too," she whispered. "And by the way, you're returning this as soon as the round is over."

"No way," I said as I kissed her, and walked quickly back to my ball.

You'd think I'd have been distracted by all this, but it was the opposite. I had never been more focused in my life. Without taking a second peek at the line or another practice stroke, I dropped my putter behind the ball. I set my feet.

Then I let it go.

I didn't even look to see what happened. I didn't have to. I was a fool in love, who was loved in return. The instant I hit it, I knew it was dead center, and that I was in a three-way tie for the lead of the U.S. Senior Open with Jack Nicklaus and Raymond Floyd. As the gallery erupted and sprinted to the final tee, Earl slapped me on the shoulder and said, "Travis, my friend, it's a real good thing you sunk that putt. Because if you hadn't, you'd be carrying this bag right now."

I peeked behind me and saw Sarah and the kids jumping up and down, inventing the McKinley jig.

Thank God, I said to myself.

So, it's not a dream.

They're actually here.

And so am I.

Chapter 36

I can't deny I felt a certain glow as I walked to the 18th hole. But I was also feeling like I was being wheeled into some foreign city's emergency room at three in the morning.

My body was numb and there was a heat blister on my brain.

My back felt like one of those vast quadruple knots in Noah's shoelaces.

My stomach was a disaster.

I had tunnel vision and cold sweats, and I was starting to see things that I hope weren't really there — like my fifth-grade science teacher, Evelyn Kochanski, sunbathing naked along the left side of the fairway.

None of this was relieved by the fact that the par-5 18th at Pebble Beach, with the Pacific running the entire left side of the hole, is the most frightening finishing hole in golf. Hook the ball off the tee, something I'm particularly adept at, and the only thing that can save you is the Coast Guard.

For reasons I'll never understand, I hit a perfect drive, as did my co-leaders, and since none of us could reach the green in two, all I wanted to do with my second shot was advance the ball up the right side with a nice little 5-iron. No sweat.

As I started my backswing, I thought: *Smooth and easy.*

Then I thought: *Miss it anywhere but left.*

Then my grandfather screeched (inside my head, I hope): *One swing thought!* Which unfortunately was my third swing thought.

The result of all this complex thought was a wicked shank slice that scattered the gallery and rolled to a stop among a thick stand of pines on the right side of the fairway at least 275 yards from the green.

I felt like digging a shallow grave and throwing myself in.

Instead, I looked over at Simon, and he looked like he was taking it even harder than me.

So did Elizabeth and Pop.

But then I caught the eye of Noah, who offered one of his "Oh, well, what are you going to do?" shrugs.

And as usual, the little gink was right. Whatever happened was going to happen, and besides it was only golf. The 18th hole was important, but it wasn't that important.

And standing right behind him, Sarah held up her new ring, and she mouthed "It's beautiful!"

I headed toward the trees to find my damn ball.

Chapter 37

I knew it wasn't going to be pretty when I spotted Rosi gingerly hovering over my ball as if it were a radioactive turd, shaking his head and whispering into his headset in hushed, funereal tones. However, as soon as Earl and I got close enough to survey the damage ourselves, I saw that I wasn't dead. I was just screwed.

There's a difference.

Although there was a stand of hearty pines rooted between my ball and the fairway, there was a small gap, no more than a yard square, between the third and fourth trees, and if I could somehow hit a hard low draw through the hole, I could not only get back to the fairway, I could hit it at the green.

To say that it was unlikely I could poke a full-throttle drive through an opening the size of a small window is putting it politely. But with

Jack and Raymond both sitting pretty in the center of the fairway less than a hundred yards from the flag, chipping it sideways would have been tantamount to surrender anyway.

I figured I might as well scare a few trees first.

Now I know I've already used up more than my quota of miracles in this story. In fact, I probably had to use a couple of yours, too. So I won't categorize what happened next as yet another piece of divine intervention. Let's just call it the greatest shot in golf history, and leave it at that.

With the gallery rubbernecking with morbid delight, I pulled back my driver and swung at that ball as if I were wielding a sledgehammer at a county fair. When all I heard were gasps, I knew that sucker was rocketing toward the green.

In fact, I was a little disappointed when I raced back to the fairway and discovered that the ball had stopped rolling a couple of yards short on a little knoll.

Raymond Floyd was next, and with a wristy flourish he lofted a wedge that covered the flag the whole way. The shot stopped on a dime six feet from the hole.

Jack's approach was even prettier, so pretty that as it dropped out of the sky my heart dropped with it, and I turned to Earl and said, "We're going to lose on a slam dunk."

"No, we're not," he replied, never taking his eyes from the ball.

An instant later the ball struck the cup or the flag, or the point where the cup and the flag came together, and struck it so cleanly that the ball bounced almost thirty feet away on the slick green.

"Son-of-a-bitch hit it too pure!" said Earl appreciatively.

Chapter 38

I hope that all of you, at least once in your life, get the chance to walk up the 18th fairway of Pebble Beach with Jack Nicklaus and Raymond Floyd, on a perfect July afternoon, tied for the lead in the final round of the U.S. Senior Open.

It's a lot of fun.

By the time we reached the green, every spectator who had come out for the final round was standing on the bank between the hole and the clubhouse, and they were going apeshit. Times Square on V-E Day, Woodstock when the rain stopped, and the ticker tape parade for the '69 Mets must have felt something like this. In all the excitement, I may even have doffed my hat.

The only person who wasn't delighting in the ecstatic suspense was Jack Nicklaus, who had just hit three perfect golf shots and was away.

After caroming off the stick and cup, Nicklaus's ball had rolled more than thirty feet to the base of the green, and now as Jack, wearing a yellow cashmere sweater and powder blue slacks, circled his double-breaking uphill putt, surveying it from every angle except from beneath the ground, his face was locked in a deep scowl of concentration.

He really did look like a bear, a very pissed-off bear, who had just caught somebody trying to steal his honey pot. As Nicklaus stalked, the crowd grew quieter and quieter, and when he finally stepped up and rapped it firmly toward the hole, the collective tension of twenty thousand mute, stone-still golf fans dying to explode was almost unbearable.

For the second time in a row, Nicklaus aimed his ball straight and true, and this time when I turned to Earl in despair, he didn't bother to contradict me.

Like everyone else who was there, he just tilted forward and stared slack-jawed as the ball rolled inexorably toward the hole. With the bloodchilling vividness of an unwelcome flashback, I replayed in my mind Nicklaus's immortal squat and charge at the Masters in '86, when he had sunk that huge putt on 15, and raced off the green, his putter shimmering overhead in the dying afternoon light like a cavalry saber.

The putt barreled holeward, dead center all the way. I braced myself for yet another Nicklaus sprint into history, recalling in that gloomy instant the often-forgotten fact that, in addition to being a golfing prodigy, young Jack was the Ohio high school champion in the 100-yard dash.

I had no right to complain. It had been a great ride. Better than great.

But now it was over. The fat lady was about to sing. Jack dropped into his standing crouch. It was in!

Until it screeched to a stop on the lip, half a turn short.

The crowd exhaled.

So did I.

Jack tapped in for par.

Chapter 39

My own Titleist 3, the sole survivor of the sleeve Pop had dropped on the grass the week before in Winnetka, was sparkling on the slope five feet off the green, twenty-five feet from the hole, with the green running sharply downhill away from me.

It was the kind of chip you definitely wouldn't want if you had to make par. But for a golfer on the verge of a nervous breakdown who needed a birdie, it was a chip with possibilities. For one thing, it was physically impossible to leave the ball short.

Choking up — no pun intended — on a 9-iron, I set the blade behind the ball, then gave it the gentlest of flicks. I watched as the ball barely cleared the rough and bounced softly on the green. I watched it steadily put on more and more speed. Then I watched it *dive* like Bugs Bunny into the back of the hole. *At least that's what I think I saw.*

Everything went sideways. Twenty thousand people leaped toward the sky, and I fell to my knees, where Earl got down with me and gave me a hug I swear I can still feel. For several minutes, the world was nothing but noise.

Finally the roar began to subside, and I stood up and walked to the hole to pluck out my ball. But before I retrieved my ball, I did something I hadn't done in eighteen holes.

I looked over at Raymond and I stared straight into his eyes.

And I winked.

Now, it's one thing having to sink a six-footer on the last hole of the U.S. Senior Open to force a play-off with Jack Nicklaus, the holder of twenty major titles and the greatest golfer to ever trod the sod. It's quite another having to sink a six-footer to avoid losing to Travis McKinley, an unknown rookie, who had never won a single full-length sanctioned event in his life, and six months earlier was squeezing out bad advertising jingles. As Floyd stepped up to his putt, he was fighting more pressure than any competitive psyche should ever be asked to handle.

But if Raymond was feeling the heat, he wasn't sharing that fact with me or anyone else. As I'd seen so many times before on TV, he strutted up to his ball with brisk, officious little steps, wiggled his butt into a comfortable position, and with his lips slightly pursed, squinted back and forth between the ball and the cup as if he couldn't quite decide which of the two was a bigger asshole.

He looked composed, and focused, and utterly unflappable. He looked like a contract killer taking care of business. Then he yanked that six-footer so far left that *it missed the hole by half a foot*.

Suddenly, I had Sarah, Simon, Noah, and Elizabeth in my arms. I was dancing with Pop and then with Earl, and then I think Earl had all of us in his arms. I was shaking hands with Raymond Floyd and Jack Nicklaus, and then I was giving the winning golf ball back to my grandfather. "Thanks for the loan, Pop," I shouted through the roar. "Now don't hit this one in a lake."

"Don't worry," he said, beaming even more brightly than usual, "I'll just use it for chipping."

And somewhere in the basement of the Pebble Beach clubhouse, a lonely jeweler began scratching "T. McKinley" on a very large silver cup.

Post-Miracle
Happenings

Two months later.

Two in the morning.

A dream stirs me from a deep sleep, and I sit up in a large oak bed where, in an odd way, I feel completely comfortable for the first time.

As my eyes adjust to the moonlight, I scan a room that is both familiar and brilliantly new. On one side is an old wooden chest I inherited from my great-grandfather. On the right is a chest and mirror that Sarah got from her grandmother, with inlaid flowers on the doors, and a large lacquer tray resting on top filled with tortoiseshell combs and a pair of antique Russian silver bracelets she has been wearing for more than twenty years.

Although I'd only been gone about six months, I have no trouble imagining how Odysseus must have felt to be finally back home with Penelope after a ten-year trek through the world.

Careful not to wake Sarah, who lies on her side facing me, the slightest trace of a smile curling the edges of her small mouth, I slide out of bed and wander through my old house, a house my grandfather built, with the help of only a single laborer, the year I was born.

Even though she hasn't lived at home for half a dozen years now, I visit Elizabeth's room first. With its fading rock star posters still taped to the wall, and its stuffed animals, it looks like a kind of teenage time capsule, circa 1984. Earnest, irreproachable Elizabeth, who in twenty-seven years never gave us a thing to worry about. Was she ever really a teenager, or did she go directly from infancy to radiology? It occurs to me that I know less about her than my other children. The next morning I will call Elizabeth to schedule a trip to New Haven to try to do something about that.

Then I lean into Simon's room, and see him peacefully stretched out, three earrings and all, his thin, six-two frame hanging over the edges of his ten-year-old single bed. You can't love any one of your kids more than another, and I swear to God I don't. But for better and worse, Simon is me, and my heart feels so connected to his that it doesn't even have to go out to him. It's already there.

Lying beside him like a faithful little pup, or better yet, like a not-to-be-underestimated watchdog, his oversized shaggy brown head resting on Simon's back, is our own great man Noah, who must have been feeling restless himself and wandered to his brother's room in the middle of the night. Noah, the third and final member of this small generation of McKinleys. The miracle kid, whose arrival itself was a surprise and who has been startling us in one way or another ever since. But then again, *as Lee said*, and I call him Lee now, even in my mind, we're all miracles out here, every last one of us.

I carefully pick Noah up, and deposit him back in his own bed, in his own room across the hall. Then I take a seat in the living room, and sit there for a good long while in the dim light, just drinking it all in.

Sarah. Elizabeth. Simon. Noah. Sarah. Elizabeth. Simon. Noah.

I sit there until I catch my own smiling reflection in a large silver bowl on the mantel above the fireplace, and then I wander back to my own bed.

If I'm not the happiest man alive, God bless whoever is.

One last thing.

That following Christmas morning I went out to play golf again.

It wasn't anything I'd planned on doing, but when I stepped outside that morning to scrape the *Tribune* off the stoop, and saw that even at eight in the morning the temperature was already in the high teens, it just seemed like the right thing to do, if only as a way of showing my gratitude for the whole chain of events last year's round had set off.

Once again Christmas caught the Chicago winter napping — the mercury continued to soar throughout the morning — and by the time I pulled my big burgundy Beemer into the Creekview Country Club a little past noon — the temperature was a balmy 34 degrees. For some time, I just stood by my car in the empty lot, stretching and thinking in the steep light. I was like a seal sunning himself on an ice floe.

Finally, I headed to the 17th tee, and as I bent over to thumb my tee into the resistant turf, I caught a wave of déjà vu so powerful it almost knocked me over.

As I started to play, it only grew more intense.

Hadn't my first drive last year come to rest beside the very same sprinkler head? Didn't my 5-iron check up on this exact spot on the green? Haven't I seen that skinny red squirrel somewhere before?

Once again, I stood over a nine-foot eagle putt on the 17th green. Once again I saw the line as clearly as if it had been stenciled on the short grass. Once again I poured it dead center into the back of the cup.

And once again, I played or replayed, however you want to put it, the round of my life. If anything, I played a little better this time out, because after a year on tour and a lot of help from Earl, I wasn't quite so unnerved by being a few strokes under par.

But this was more than a few strokes under par. Eagles weren't an endangered species in Chicago that Christmas — I had two in the first four holes — and by the time I made the turn, I knew in my bones I was going to break the course record of 62, a mark I'd been chasing since my grandfather brought me to this course almost half a century ago.

With only 15 and 16 left to play (remember, I started on 17), I was already eleven under par. To break the record, all I had to do was par out. Then I birdied 15. Now all I had to do was bogey 16, and 16 is the shortest and easiest par 4 on the course.

Whistling like Fuzzy, I bent over to tee up my final drive of the year.

But as I stood back up, a strong gust lifted my Pebble Beach cap into the wind, and when I spun to snatch it back, I saw the same Christmas display tethered to a nearby house that had snapped me out of my reverie the year before.

Once again, it sent me fishing for my watch in a panic.

When I read the time, I had the urge to drop to my knees and kiss the semifrozen Winnetka dirt. I had spent a lot more time stretching than I thought. Maybe I even zoned out there for a while. But even if I ran into a parade and caught every red light in town, I could still walk into my house with plenty of time to shower and shave before Christmas dinner.

In fact, I could probably finish my round and still get home on time.

But I'd be cutting it close.

I didn't even bend down to pick up my ball. I just threw my bag over my shoulder, and started running for dear life.